CYBORG FEVER

CYBORG FEVER

LAURIE SHECK

TUPELO PRESS
NORTH ADAMS, MA

Cyborg Fever

ISBN 978-1-961209-26-8 (paper)
ISBN 978-1-961209-51-0 (eBook)

Library of Congress Cataloging-in-Publication Data
Names: Sheck, Laurie, author.
Title: Cyborg fever / Laurie Sheck.
Description: First paperback edition. | North Adams, MA : Tupelo Press, 2025. | Summary: "Cyborg Fever is a moving and lyrical exploration of what it means to be human and to love in the age of AI and increasing transhumanism."-- Provided by publisher.
Identifiers: LCCN 2024054304 | ISBN 9781961209268 (paperback)
Subjects: LCGFT: Fiction.
Classification: LCC PS3569.H3917 C93 2025 | DDC 813/.54--dc23/eng/20241125
LC record available at https://lccn.loc.gov/2024054304

Text Design by Allison O'Keefe
Cover Art: Photo by CHUTTERSNAP on Unsplash
First paperback edition: June 2025

Tupelo Press
P.O. Box 1767
North Adams, Massachusetts 01247
(413) 664-9611 / Fax: (413) 664-9711
editor@tupelopress.org / www.tupelopress.org

Tupelo Press is an award-winning independent literary press that publishes fine fiction, non-fiction, and poetry in books that are a joy to hold as well as read. Tupelo Press is a registered 501(c)(3) non-profit organization, and we rely on public support to carry out our mission of publishing extraordinary work that may be outside the realm of the large commercial publishers. Financial donations are welcome and are tax deductible.

NATIONAL ENDOWMENT for the ARTS arts.gov

This project is supported in part by an award from the National Endowment for the Arts.

TABLE OF CONTENTS

I. ENTROPY

1. Entropy

The mathematical definition of entropy, S=k log W, is inscribed on the gravestone of Ludwig Boltzmann, the renowned Austrian physicist who hung himself in Duino, Italy, in 1906.

This inscription was among his last wishes.

He had devoted his life to the atomic theory of matter, and to the idea that the universe moves toward increasing chaos and disorder.

All this I learned from Funes during the long, black year of my fever. Out of the darkness, I could see him bathed in the white glow of his computer, I could see what he was reading and writing. Sometimes his screen glowed with what he read, at others with what he wrote, I couldn't always tell the difference. Sometimes his lips moved, but I never heard him speak. Where was he? Where was I? I didn't know. All I knew was he was on a narrow cot in a small room where he chain-smoked and read, and his legs couldn't move.

Funes knew so many things, sometimes it seemed he knew almost everything. The workings of the stars. If a void is really empty. The 600 known species of the genus Passiflora. The precise number of times, 7,637, the word sun appears in several obscure, ancient texts. Various theories about black holes, dark energy, dark matter.

Often I didn't see him for weeks at a time, but always he came back.

Ludwig Boltzmann said every molecular structure, no matter how large or small, is pulled toward formlessness and isolation. Everything in the universe is moving away from everything else. Nothing ever moves in the opposite direction. One day the stars will be so far away there will be only blackness.

Funes found this both beautiful and lonely.

Ludwig Boltzmann's grave is in *Zentralfriedholf*, Vienna's largest and most famous cemetery. Grave 1, Group 14c, not far from the graves of Beethoven and Brahms. The graves of Schoenberg, Schubert and Strauss are also nearby, as is the grave of August Zang, the originator of the French croissant.

Though Funes could never go there, he still knew the directions. Visitors could reach the cemetery by trams 71 and 6, bus number 171, or the Schnellbahn S7 train.

His face seemed almost to soften as he typed this. As if he were touching something kind and tender on the Earth, something true, benevolent, unconflicted. Of which, he made clear, there was little.

Ludwig Boltzmann was subject to drastic mood swings which he sometimes blamed on being born on the night between Mardi Gras and Ash Wednesday, but which, in darker moods, he attributed to the dismissal and mockery of his ideas, his increasing isolation.

He wrote *The Kinetic Theory of Gases*, and published numerous scientific papers. Some called him *the man who loved atoms.*

In the weeks before his death, he said, *It is very beautiful in Duino at the end of summer, by the sea.*

Funes said he possessed the beauty of the antiparticle. It was his highest compliment.

He reserved it for Boltzmann, for Nikola Tesla, a few others.

The antiparticle has no place on this Earth. Its existence depends on its apartness. Particles and antiparticles annihilate on contact.

But once it was different.

In the earliest moments of the universe, out of the blasting heat of explosion, radiant energy created particles and antiparticles in equal number, and they moved together in a vast sea of disturbance and collision. But as the universe cooled and expanded, a kind of broken symmetry occurred, leaving slightly more particles than antiparticles, and making possible our world of matter. (Those particles shimmer even now within the stars of fifty billion galaxies). After that, it was hard to find any antiparticles at all.

But where could they have gone to? How could they just vanish like that? How could half the universe go missing? And with no trace, no explanation.

As if to exist is a hiddenness, opaque and secret.

Like the violent, invisible quietness of skin.

These things I learned in the white glow of Funes' computer.

Ludwig Boltzmann died 22 years before Paul Dirac made his equation affirming the existence of antimatter, and 26 years before Carl Anderson saw a track of electrons, each accompanied by a matching particle of the opposite charge, emerging from cosmic showers in a cloud chamber.

These particles of opposite charge that, if they touched even slightly, would immediately destroy each other.

In his increasing isolation, Boltzmann devoted the last years of his life to the study of the probability of disorder and found a strange beauty in how molecular structures, no matter how small, contain the potential for a vast profusion of possibilities, though all move in the direction of chaos, dissolution.

"Entropy is the measure of the degree of randomness and disorder in a closed and changing system."

It is said Paul Dirac was an unusually quiet man, and his colleagues coined the term *dirac* to indicate a speaking rate of one word per hour.

The one time he is said to have showed emotion was when he cried at the news of Einstein's death.

When asked to speak about his equation proving the existence of antimatter he simply said, "I think it is beautiful."

"Beauty," Werner Heisenberg said, "is the proper conformity of the parts to one another and to the whole."

And Francis Bacon said, "There is no excellent beauty that does not have some strangeness in the proportion."

I thought about Francis Bacon's definition.

How Funes was beautiful to me, though his fingers were yellowed with nicotine, and his legs didn't move. As if he had taken into himself the secret hurts of the world, its troubled angles.

Nikola Tesla could hear the ticking of a watch three rooms away. A fly alighting on a table caused a dull thud in his ear. He felt a violent aversion toward women's earrings. The shrill whistle from a distant locomotive scorched his inner ear like burning coals. The sight of a pearl was unbearable. He couldn't stand to touch human hair and never would "except perhaps at the point of a revolver." He grew feverish from looking at a peach.

He pondered the mysterious injury inside each human body. Its delicate, indescribable beauty.

The secrets of the universe will be found in energy, frequency, vibration.

Alternate currents pass with astonishing freedom through rarefied gasses.

He believed the Earth is a charged body once companioned by other oppositely electrified bodies from which it became separated long ago. It has lost its sense of belonging.

We cannot understand the life of a crystal but it is nonetheless a living being.

He said a single ray of light from a distant star falling upon the eye of a tyrant in bygone times may have altered the course of the tyrant's life, and so changed the destiny of nations.

All things are particles of a real and rhythmic whole.

One day the wireless transmission of intelligence will throb beneath the ocean currents.

He invented the Tesla Coil, the remote control, the laser, the Tesla valve, the induction motor. Made possible the use of alternating current. Filed over 300 patents.

"It is absolutely immaterial to me whether I run my turbine in thought or test it in my shop. There is no difference whatever; the results are the same. In this way I am able to rapidly develop and perfect a conception without touching anything. When I have gone so far as to embody every possible improvement I can think of and see no fault anywhere, I put into concrete form this product of my brain. Invariably my device works as I conceived that it should, and the experiment comes out exactly as I planned it. In twenty years there has not been a single exception."

He determined to finish anything he started which included, to his dismay, the entire works of Voltaire, one hundred volumes in small print.

He delighted in picturing motors running.

He envisioned a system that could distribute the world's music and indicate time with astronomical precision.

One day, when the air suddenly filled with an indescribably sweet song of many voices, he realized his mother had died.

Often he felt the heat of a small sun beneath his skull.

He believed the human body can feel the pain of the cosmos.

He loved a pigeon above all others.

But why was Funes learning these things? What did they mean to him? And why was I seeing him and his computer when I could see nothing else? All I knew was he was there, I could see him, and in the darkness I continued reading.

In 1903, at the age of 7, the physicist Erwin Schrodinger, vacationing with his family at the Sudbahn Hotel at the mountain resort of Semmerling, south of Vienna, was awoken by a terrifying dream which left him unable to speak. He had seen the word PRISON written in large letters on the wall beside his bed.

In the last years of his life, Paul Dirac, "looking fragile as a glass-cut figurine," called his life a failure. He spoke of the beautiful mathematics of creation, and of how in earlier years when he was at a loss how to proceed, "I would just have to wait...and the hand of mathematics would lead me along an unexpected path where new vistas opened."

But with that early work behind him, he longed for a theory explaining the interaction of electrons and protons that would stand free of "disfiguring infinities."

He never found it.

In 1940 he dismissed one equation on the grounds it was too ugly.

And in 1963 he wrote: "It is more important to have beauty in one's equations than to have them fit the experiment."

Pure thought is music.

There is a substratum of existence which is impossible to picture.

If a theory is mathematically beautiful but seems wrong, it is only because its meaning hasn't yet been grasped.

Subrahmanyan Chandrasekhar attended each of Dirac's lectures four times. He called his thought "a piece of music you want to hear over and over again," and wrote in a letter to this father, "He is meek and shy, and walks very close to the walls."

Funes lay in the white glow of his computer, his neck and back propped on pillows at one end of his cot, the silver, foldable legs of the bed-desk balanced on either side of his hips. The words moved slowly over the screen, as if thinking themselves into being, unsure if they wanted to be seen. Mostly there were facts, though now and then he typed in questions that every time I saw them made me wonder what else he was thinking that I'd never guess—*What percentage of reality is visible? What role does the ankle dorsiflexor muscle play in the modulation and control of human walking? If there is a ghost in the machine, what happens to the ghost when the machine is destroyed?* And all the while I watched him, I didn't know where I was, or where he was.

Having lost his financial backing and living in near-total isolation, Nikola Tesla occupied himself with the wireless transmission of energy. He envisioned an electric wave moving freely over the Earth effecting the flow of time and altering the inertia and movement of mind and body. Each object in the world, however small, is matter and force governed by law.

Impressed by Helmholtz's experiments with sight, he called them "beautiful" and wrote of how "the fundi of the eye are themselves luminous...Helmholtz could see, in total darkness, the movement of his arm by the light of his own eyes."

The body is a site of justice and radiance.

One must follow "a departure from known methods."

"I purpose to show that, however impossible it may now seem, an automaton may be contrived which will have its own mind."

He kept open his hotel room windows for the pigeons in Bryant Park which he fed each day and often a second time at night. He stored casks of seeds and hung basket nests for the ones that came inside. He nursed wing diseases, broken legs, gangrene.

One night, when "solving problems as usual" he looked up and saw the white pigeon with touches of grey on her wings, the one he loved, fly in through the open window and stand on his desk. He understood she came to tell him she was dying.

He held her through the night, and when she died the next morning he sensed his work was finished.

From that day forward, on the rare occasion an acquaintance approached him on the street, he simply said, "You may leave me now."

"No matter how vanishingly small, each separate thing is in itself a world, a whole universe..."

On its editorial page, *The Herald Tribune* criticized him for interrupting his scientific work "with daily walks to Bryant Park to feed the silly and inconsequential pigeons."

But my friend, what can quell this overwhelming disquiet at the riddle that we are here, that the world is as it is, that it is incomprehensible? The laws of thought must be broken. Many still believe that Euclid's geometry alone is possible, that the sum of the angles in a triangle must be 180 degrees, that there is no such thing as four dimensional space. But the Earth turning on an axis was also once thought absurd. Would a landscape on Mars or on a planet off Sirius really not exist if no living being was ever able to perceive them?

The train is arriving, I will write more later. It is only a short journey from Bremen to Vienna.

Yours,
Ludwig Boltzmann

To Nikola Tesla nothing on Earth was inconsequential, beneath notice, without meaning.

Contrary to the Herald Tribune, what at first appears trivial may be revealed to be ingenious.

Humility is the heart of seeing.

Inconsequential was first recorded as an adjective in English in 1615. In Hindi, it is *kramarahit*. In Tamil, *arra*.

What is logic but a defense against a different kind of knowing? Untamed, anarchic.

"How subtle are the influences that shape our destiny. As a boy I watched a snowball enlarge into an avalanche, and ever since the magnification of feeble actions fascinates me."

"Many technical men, very able in their specialized departments but near-sighted and dominated by a pedantic spirit, have asserted that excepting the induction motor, I have given the world little of practical use. This is a grievous mistake. A new idea must not be judged by its immediate result."

"I am unwilling to accord to some smallminded and jealous individuals the satisfaction of having thwarted my efforts. These men are to me nothing more than microbes of a nasty disease. My project was too far ahead of time. The world was not prepared for it. But the same laws will prevail in the end and make it a triumphal success."

"When a child, I found I could harness the energies of nature through May bugs. These small creatures were remarkably efficient, for once they were started, they had no sense to stop and continued whirling for hours and hours and the hotter it was the harder they labored."

"There is no empty dreaming."

The blackness of my fever moved in slow, gentle waves around me. I realized I had drifted away from Earth—that I, too, was a wave, swelling and ebbing, diffuse and quiet.

Funes was all I had left of the world.

It seemed he and his small room with its glowing computer were drifting through the blackness, too.

And as I drifted, shards of memory came back to me. How I was a boy in an orphanage—had lived there all my life—and one day the director, the only guardian I'd ever known and who I'd grown to love, suddenly refused to speak to me or even look in my direction. Her name was Sister Gudrun.

I tried to figure out what terrible thing I must have done. Several times each week she'd taken me to a book-lined room where she read, and I listened. We sat side by side by the tall window. But now she was a pool of black water, and no matter how much I blamed myself and wondered, I didn't know why.

Suddenly I was alone. Lost, forsaken.

Darkly in her long black dress and heavy shoes, she paced in slow circles in the courtyard and acted like she didn't see me.

My skin was flashes of heat and cold. After a few days I couldn't make myself eat, my shirt hung loosely from my shoulders. A black sun beat in my chest.

I remembered something else. Around that time, a man and woman stopped visiting me on weekends. Up until that time I believed they were going to adopt me. They were kind and patient. Sometimes they took me to the park by the river. I even saw them in Sister Gudrun's office signing papers. But then she stopped speaking to me and I never saw them again.

As the days of her silence continued, I felt strangely heavy and light at the same time. It was a feeling like the sadness of gravity. At night black flowers tall as poles gathered at my bedside. They asked me in the language of flowers if my parents named me. I said I didn't know. This seemed to hurt them.

Soon my fever hurled me from the world.

I couldn't understand what had happened to me, why I was suddenly alone.

Nicolaus Cusanus said we are like night owls trying to look at the sun. The more we seek to understand the universe, the more it withdraws from us. And Anaxagoras said, reality is mostly closed to us, all we can have of it is glimpses.

Even the plainest facts are shadows.

But even if facts are shadows, without Funes' facts, what would have become of me? In the dark solitude of my fever, I had nothing else to hold onto.

I could feel them inside me.

As his computer screen glowed, in the blackness of interstellar space, a passionflower opened.

The fever when it came was beautiful, malicious, wave-like, intrepid. A thing that loved me. Thief of gravity, of reason. Far planets glittered inside it, and black holes that signaled a deep peace or terror— I couldn't tell which one, or was it both. I lay in its vast solitude until landlessness was the only truth, each wave a questioning and wound. The universe is dark energy, dark matter, I knew this, it is everything we can't know or understand. I moved inside it, a small speck of materiality, a figment, a delusion, almost-nothing. The fever was waves of the real, of the exact and brutal, the scarring and the scarred. It knew about the thoughts I had, the books I'd read. Sometimes it sent them washing over me, over my lit skin or was I gauze by then or air or nothing. The blackness shifted to degrees of gray, then shifted back, the light kept decohering. The Earth was near then very far, a mute helplessness revolving. Mostly I couldn't see it at all. Far away, the orphanage was still standing, its walls unwavering and strong. It is a fact of this Earth some children are born unwanted, uncared for, I was one...I understood I was not unusual, it happened from the beginning of time and would happen until the end of time... Even planets are hurled from their orbits, sometimes they drifted past me in their cauls of ice, lightless and alone without sunrise or sunset...I wanted to touch them but I never could. And all the while something beat inside me, a narrow want, a pulsing. The black waves kept coming... There are special glasses being developed that are programmed to show you what you want what you can live with—I had learned this—They show 3D movies and take you away to far-off places, you can see what you want to you don't have to face what's real— but the fever didn't know this. It kept filling with black holes, lost planets.

The last story Sister Gudrun ever read to me was *Funes the Memorias* by Jorge Luis Borges.

She said Borges was a blind librarian, Director of the National Library of Argentina, and that the library's two previous directors also had gone blind. One, Paul Grossac, loved the library so deeply even in his final illness he refused to leave it and died in his office behind the large mahogany u-shaped desk.

In the story, Ireneo Funes lives with his mother, a laundress, in the town of Fray Bentos, in Uruguay, in a small house with a fig tree in the garden. Some say his father is the doctor in the salting house (in which case he is an Englishman) but others claim he is an oxcart driver, or a breaker of horses.

Ireneo Funes doesn't know his father.

Even as a child, he possesses unusual powers. He can tell the exact time without looking at a watch or the sun's position. ("What's the time, Ireneo? Four minutes till eight, young Bernardo Juan Francisco.") The narrator calls him *chronometric Funes.*

But at the age of 19, a fall from a half-broken horse leaves him permanently crippled.

From that day on, he lies on a narrow cot in the laundress's back room, chain smoking and reading. Sometimes he fixes his eyes on a spiderweb in a corner, or the fig tree in the garden. But a strange thing begins to happen, though his legs are immobilized, his mind is flying. He can remember everything— every cloud in the sky on the morning of April 30, 1882, every crack in the binding of a book glanced at just once.

His own hands and face surprise him every time he sees them in a mirror. He realizes no two moments are exactly alike. A dog seen in profile at 3:13 p.m. is in no way equivalent to the same dog seen at 3:45 in a different position. “He saw—he noticed—the progress of death, of humidity. He was the solitary spectator of a multiform, almost unbearably precise world.” Every second of every day he feels “the heat and pressure of reality.” Nothing is too minute or unimportant. Anything he sees or learns he can never forget.

He teaches himself English, French, Portuguese, Latin.

Often he longs to rest his eyes, to be oblivious for even just a little while. At nights he imagines himself at the bottom of a river, rocked and negated by the current.

How much shadow can be piled upon shadow, how much light upon countless memories of light?

In a moment of bitterness, he compares his mind to a garbage heap. But when he holds a passionflower in his hand, he sees it as no one ever saw it before.

At the rare times a visitor comes, he might let himself be carried at dusk to the window.

He lives this way for several years. At the age of 22, he dies of pulmonary congestion.

In the silence after the story's final word, the crumbled light on Sister Gudrun's cheek was wild and ashen as the surface of the moon. I hadn't known a story could be so beautiful without being beautiful. That a Funes, a creature of the Earth like me, bookish and quiet like me, could feel so close and yet I'd never met him.

Funes had died, but I felt his heartbeat pulsing over mine. I had never felt another's heartbeat before. It seemed a small, blind animal, exposed and unprotected, and that many things could hurt it. I wished I could look after it, though I knew I couldn't. In my mind, I still saw the pile of books beside his bed, the ashtray filled with cigarette butts, the fig tree, the dried sprig of artemisia, his ruined legs, the barred window.

Even though Funes had died, his heart was beating. I understood this couldn't be possible, but it was. Sister Gudrun was still there beside me. And now, in the darkness of my fever, I was surprised to find Funes hadn't vanished, though his room was different—there was no barred window, no garden, and it couldn't still be 1889—it was lit with incandescent light and he read on a computer.

Holderlin said he had many songs but they were stolen from him and devoured by sadness. He said we are nothing, what we search for is everything. Now that Funes couldn't go to the world, it seemed he could still search for it, and the world could come to him. In the darkness of my need, I found him.

Bathed in computer-light, Funes' body was white and shadowed as the moon. On the floor beside his cot, his ash tray overflowed with ash and cigarette butts. Every now and then he lifted his knees with both hands to adjust his lifeless legs, or reached for his pack of cigarettes and matches. As I watched him move his silent lips, he was a theremin the wind was playing, though it never touched him, its music lost and distant as the stars.

Funes' screen filled again with words:

As a child, Ludwig Boltzmann learned to play the piano and played throughout his life. His teacher was Anton Bruckner.

Nikola Tesla was forbidden to learn a musical instrument or to play cards. Nevertheless, in 1921, when the Russian scientist Leon Theremin was experimenting with the Tesla Coil, he found that depending on his proximity, it would hum at different pitches. From this he invented the theramin, the only musical instrument played without being touched.

There is also the Singing Tesla Coil, a form of plasma speaker whose sounds are square-like waveforms.

When asked if he played a musical instrument, Paul Dirac replied plainly "I do not know. I have never tried."

Acrobatic, Wolfgang Pauli described Dirac's way of theorizing.

Although Dirac grew up in England, his father insisted he speak French, and refused to reply if his son spoke English. This caused him to say as little as possible and only when absolutely necessary.

His silence was a form of music.

After reading Dirac's articles, Einstein said he trod the narrow path between genius and madness.

Rudolf Clausius devised the Clausius-Clapeyron equation describing the phase transition between two planes of matter that have the same composition. Maybe this is a kind of music.

Using a technique called magneto-seismology, solar physicists in Sheffield, England recorded musical sounds made by the movement of magnetic loops within the Sun's corona.

It is said the solar atmosphere is constantly pervaded by coronal music.

"My house is on fire but you are like Bismarck, great but uncontrollable," Nikola Tesla wrote to J.P. Morgan after Morgan's refusal to fund the completion of Wardenclyffe Tower, Tesla's wireless transmission station in Shoreham, Long Island.

He had broken his rule of writing letters only on the 13th of each month. This left him in a fever.

"I will harness the sun's energy, control the weather with electricity, and war will become a thing of the past."

To the industrialist Henry O. Havemeyer, Tesla sent a gift of a cabochon sapphire ring, but Havermeyer also turned him down.

The Earth is made of beautiful disturbances. There will be no need for artificial conductors.

The charged upper layers of the atmosphere will be used to light cities and shipping lanes at night.

Signals are born of disruption and economy.

Wardenclyffe's proposed design included a laboratory, instrumentation room, machine shop, library, and a glass-blowing site for the making of tubes and bulbs.

When asked by reporters what he was building, Tesla replied, "I cannot say at present."

In 1902, after a year of construction, the tower reached 187 feet, its full height.

It is said on the eve of J.P. Morgan's refusal, it came alive with shooting sparks that sent flashes of light through the sky.

In 1917, George C. Bolt, the proprietor of the Waldorf Astoria Hotel, foreclosed on the property and on July 4, the Smiley Steel Company began Wardenclyffe's demolition.

The scrap value was listed at $1,750.00

After that, Tesla became bedridden with a mysterious illness. When finally he was well again, he spent many hours in a makeshift laboratory in New York City, wrapping himself in electrical wire he shot through with currents of such intensity they danced and melted on his body.

“Out of the many thousands of pigeons I fed and cared for, there was one I loved above all others. She was white with light gray wing-tips, and no matter where I was, I had only to wish for her and soon she would come flying. I loved her as a man loves a woman, and she loved me. If I needed her or she needed me, nothing else mattered. As long as I had her, there was purpose to my life.”

But unlike Tesla, it seemed Funes had no one. As he lay alone in his room, he couldn’t know I watched him.

Paul Dirac disliked being photographed. If a reporter came looking for him, he pretended he was not Paul Dirac but an "ordinary citizen."

He believed beauty is the lodestar of fundamental theories of nature, and each subsequent theory should be more beautiful than the one preceding it.

For many years he lived with the misconception that men spoke French and women spoke English.

After several decades of supervising PhD theses, he suddenly inquired, "What is supervision?"

He felt a hatred for the infinities present in his own equations describing electron-photon interactions, and believed one day a theory showing them as finite would be found. But he could not find it.

In the last paper he ever wrote, he called his theory "fundamentally flawed" and encouraged those who came after to go beyond it.

Beauty is the only teacher.

All truth is beauty.

As the words appeared on Funes' screen, often I wondered, was he choosing them, or did they choose him? What need and longing drew him to Tesla's love for the white pigeon with gray wing-tips, to antiparticles, entropy, Paul Dirac's questions, coronal music? If these were the shapes and echoes of his loneliness, was he trying to answer the problem of who he was, what he longed for, what might become of him? How it felt to be immobile and alone? Could he be in a fever like mine?

Maybe the words on the screen were his self-portrait.

I still wished that I could feel his heartbeat.

When Ludwig Boltzmann was 15, Charles Darwin published *Origin of Species*. A decade later, Georg Cantor, the Russian-born mathematician who would later go mad, published his work on set theory, showing there is not just one infinity but many, and of different sizes.

Since childhood he loved the idea of the infinite. It made him happy.

He said, "The essence of mathematics is freedom."

By then, the Austro-Hungarian Empire was beginning to crack. All the supposedly God-given certainties going up in smoke.

"The infinite is everywhere. The least particle is full of an infinity of different creatures."

"A set is Many that allows itself to be thought of as One."

"The fear of infinity destroys the possibility of seeing."

His ideas were a field of wildflowers blooming very suddenly all at once, several trains speeding along the same track at the same time.

Henri Poincare labelled them a "grave disease." Leopold Kronecker called him "a charlatan, a renegade, a corrupter of youth," and made sure he would never teach in Berlin.

Gosta Mittag-Leffler, editor of *Acta Mathematica*, pulled one of his papers from the presses, saying it was "about one hundred years too soon."

Nevertheless, he found a position at the University of Halle, the only place he ever taught.

In May 1884, he suffered his first major breakdown. In a quick flurry of letters, he mentioned his nemesis Kronecker fifty-two times. "I don't know when I will be able to return to the continuation of my scientific work."

It was then he began his first confinement in the Halle Nervenklinik, the sanitarium where he spent much of the last half of his life, including in 1903 soon after the sudden death of his youngest son.

In the sanitarium he devoted himself to the study of Shakespeare.

"In the solitude of my captivity I study Shakespeare, I am sure his plays were written by Francis Bacon. Like my theory of infinite infinities, this knowledge has come to me by divine intervention. I have also been shown that Christ was the natural son of Joseph of Arimathea who implored Pontius Pilate to give him Christ's body and then prepared the tomb and buried him.

I have begged my family to take me home but they refuse. Sometimes in my dreams my son Rudolph is playing the violin with the same exquisite sweetness as his great grandfather, Franz Bohm, who was a soloist in the Russian Imperial Orchestra. But then I wake up and remember he is dead. He was always frail but had begun to grow stronger.

My theory stands firm as a rock, every arrow directed against it will return directly to its archer. I was a vessel for truth, but it brought me humiliation. Last month I wrote to the Ministry of Culture requesting I be removed from my professorship in Halle and assigned instead to the local library. This is my sincerest wish. I eagerly await their reply. So far, I have received no answer.

Kronecker says I am nothing more than an infection, but in my isolation I have followed the roots to the first infallible cause of all created things. I remember my first trip to Paris, I liked to go to the Comedie-Francaise and the Opera. I felt such joy at the idea of infinite infinities, how the universe contains unexpected and surprising freedoms."

In his later years, living in poverty, he suffered from malnutrition.

He died of a heart attack at age 72, in the Halle Nervenklinick, on January 6, 1918.

In the glow of his white room surrounded by black space, Funes held a purple passionflower in his hand. Its dark-green leaves encircled five bluish-white petals with a purple crown at the center which encircled in turn a ring of five stamens topped with five knob-like stigmas.

After a few minutes, he put it down. As his fingers moved on the keyboard, his screen filled with words, I could see him thinking:

It's said the five stamens are Jesus's wounds, the stigmas are the nails, the fringe the crown of thorns. But the suffering is invisible and has no name.

No matter how gently I hold it, its suffering will go on forever. In this way it is like Georg Cantor's infinities.

Among its common names are Passion Vine, Maycop, Maracuja. In Spanish it is *La Flor de las Cinco Lagas*. Its kingdom is Plantae, its division Magnoliophyte, its class Magnioliopsida, its order Malpighales, its family Passifloraceae, its genus Passiflora.

The motion and sensitivity of its tendrils astonished Darwin. He said a patient and astute observer could see them trembling, sensing their way forward.

In Rome, in 1609, Giacomo Bosio drew and named the parts from dried plants.

Although its cyanogenic glucosides repel most insects, the larvae of two species of butterflies, *Agraullis vanilae* and *Heliconius charitonius*, feed on its leaves—these are the only leaves they feed on.

Some have markings like clusters of eggs, a form of evolutionary protection.

Then Funes' hands stopped moving on the keyboard. His eyelids looked heavy. Maybe he felt the weight of the passionflower's scent, its unhealed wounds, the larvae's hunger.

I wished I could tell him that I was watching over him, that he could close his eyes, that he didn't need to remember Georg Cantor's infinities except when he wanted to, and even though he and I were drifting away through black space (though I didn't really know if this was true) many billions of others had done the same and were doing it right now, even if we couldn't see them. That countless passionflowers must exist in countless universes, and this seems a good thing. I wished he and I could talk about how Georg Cantor knew his idea was beautiful even if it meant he had to live his life in discouragement and in and out of a sanitarium. Even though his thoughts were seen as a grave disease, an infection.

But he didn't know I existed, we had never spoken. I watched his screen go blank. He lay his head back on the pillow and closed his eyes.

According to Konstantin Tsiolkovsky, known as the father of modern rocket science, in order for the Earth to thrive every atom must be happy.

"It is the organic need and right of all atoms not to feel torment but to exist in peace and happiness."

"When the wrong path of humanity leads it to a wild destructive state, the atoms suffer much grief. It is not only physical violence that contributes to destruction, but cunning words and thoughts imperceptible by law."

He believed for humankind to be worthy of space travel and to dwell in interstellar space, it must become more like the highly evolved inhabitants of planets that *trust the mind.*

He was said to be a happy child who flew kites and built twig huts in the forest near the small village of Izhevskoye, south of Moscow, where his father was a forester.

But at age 10, he fell ill with scarlet fever which left him hard of hearing. Because of his deafness, his school forbade him to return. "Those were the darkest years of my life. My deafness made my life uninteresting." Was it then he began to wonder about the vulnerability of the very smallest specks of matter? In what ways are they harmed? Is it possible to protect them?

He studied the few books in his father's library, made a tiny lathe, paper dirigibles, varieties of windmills, a self-propelled carriage. When he turned 16, his father sent him to Moscow to spend his days in the central library teaching himself mathematics, mechanics, physics, chemistry. Alone in his drafty room, he made experiments with quicksilver and sulphuric acid. "I remember very well I had nothing to eat but brown bread and water. Every 3 days I would buy 9 kopeks' worth of bread. I was happy with my ideas and my diet of brown bread did not dampen my spirits."

"My mind was awakened by reading."

"Left to myself, my whole life consisted of meditation, calculations, inventions, experiments. I had no one to ask if I was right or wrong. My mind was my workshop."

He began to focus on space travel. "No matter what I am doing, the idea of space flight never leaves my mind."

In 1870, he returned to his village, became a teacher of arithmetic and geometry. He remained there for the rest of his life.

All the while his experiments and theoretical inquiries continued.

Is it possible to construct gas-tight metal balloons that float eternally in the air?

Is it not possible to apply centrifugal force for lifting vehicles beyond the atmosphere out into celestial space?

"To the uninitiated, absolute phenomena appear unbelievable, magical. But they are real."

He constructed a wind tunnel to test different models of flying machines, and devised an instrument for studying the effect of the acceleration of gravity on a living organism.

He wrote over 500 scientific papers including *Dreams of the Earth and the Sky and the Effects of Universal Gravitation; Investigation of World Spaces by Reactive Vehicles; Space Rocket Trains; The Spread of Man in Space.*

He said, "The air is filled with steel birds. Gladness gives birth to kindness."

“This planet is a cradle of the human mind. But one cannot spend one’s life in a cradle.”

“It is unavoidable that we must struggle for knowledge and comfort.”

He envisioned vehicles equipped with the necessities of life permanently revolving around the Earth in a multitude of Saturn-like rings. “In all likelihood humanity will move from sun to sun as each one dies out in succession. Many decillion years hence we may be living near a sun which today exists only in embryo, in the form of nebulous matter.”

But motion in free space is impossible without the loss of matter. What fuel will be used? What is the nature of cosmic velocity?

“There was a time when to believe we could discover the composition of celestial bodies was considered senseless. At first the direct study of the universe appears even wilder—to step onto the soil of asteroids, of Mars, what could seem more extravagant?—yet in the coming era of reactive vehicles it will happen.”

“It is true no atom in the universe can avoid a difficult life. Planets and suns are destroyed, mixed, created again. Because all matter is alive, it struggles and changes. Where there is matter there is feeling. A particle of matter, of any size, feels. Nature is a continuous chain. Who can find the distinct boundary between joy and sorrow?”

An atom wanders in space, and with it, the feeling of life also wanders.

“My life has given me neither bread nor power. But I have drawn close to atoms that think and love, that live imprisoned in stone, air, water, that sleep with no awareness of time and live in the moment, that are aware of the past and paint a picture of the future, that feel pain and pleasure.”

Though there is the death of the body, atoms do not die.

In his last years he contemplated the beauty of the pursuit of light.

He left his papers to the Russian Communist Party.

He died in Kalugua, on Sept 19, 1935.

Funes rubbed his withered legs, then with both hands encircled his right knee, lifted it, put it down an inch away. Then he did the same with the left. I supposed if he lay in one position for too long, bed sores formed, maybe his disused muscles knotted and hurt him in some phantom way. All I knew for sure is once he had freedom and could move through the world, and now he couldn't. If I let myself dwell on it, it was a cruelty so blunt all mystery drained from the world, what was left was bleakness. But if I dwelled on it even longer, harder, pushed it even more, the bleakness gave way, a further mystery opened, like the wonderment and torment of Tsiolkovsky's atoms.

I'd noticed Tsiolkovsky had been bed-ridden like Funes, though much more briefly, and that as soon as he got well he began to dream of leaving Earth, immersing himself in the theories and mechanics of space travel. Having lost his freedom, all he could think of was never losing it again. But even then, he didn't forget the suffering atoms, the need to heal and protect.

I wondered if Tsiolkovsky's flight-dreams brought Funes solace. Or if, unlike me, solace had nothing to do with what he wanted.

There is a malady of the skin and blood vessels of small children that in its earliest stages moves like a soft wind through the body. The child laughs and plays as before, but something is different, and no one, not even the child, senses it is there. Several months may pass, maybe even a year. Only then do the violet heliotrope flowers appear on the child's eyelids, and the sickness makes itself known.

Sometimes the flowers cascade down the child's upper back, or form tiny clusters in the crevices between the child's fingers. The child's muscles slightly weaken. In sunlight, the petals swell and blister, so the child must learn to live in dimness and dark. It is not uncommon for the afflicted to begin to believe they don't belong in the world. And often, after a year, their hair turns silver-white like moonlight, though no one can explain why this happens.

I was six when the violet flowers appeared on my eyelids. My silver hair came later.

Nights I lay in my bed wondering why such beautiful flowers chose me for their own. Why would they want to live on the eyelids of a child? Especially a boy like me, small and quiet, without parents. What did they need from me? From the world?

I didn't understand that what was beautiful in them was also tied to secret damage.

After a while I learned the flowers are the skin rash, heliotropus myositis, named after the heliotrope that turns toward the sun (yet mine turned away), and that the heliotrope belongs to the myth of Clytie, the water nymph, lover of the sun god Helios who abandoned her to seduce the beautiful Leucothoe. After Clytie informed Leucothoe's father of his daughter's shame, he ordered Leucothoe buried alive in the sand. Shocked and remorseful at what she had done, for nine days Clytie sat on a rock, naked and wasting away. On the tenth day she became a heliotrope flower turning forever toward the sun.

Unlike Clytie, I was kept from the sun. I had no mother, no father.

I knew I would never understand the violet flowers on my eyelids, or why sunlight hurt them, or my moon-white hair when it came, or why I was an orphan.

But it wasn't the heliotrope flowers that hurled me from the world to drift through black space. Instead it was a sudden, perplexing silence, starker and more airless than the moon.

Of all the things that exist in the world, Ludwig Boltzmann felt closest to the ones he couldn't see. He deduced but couldn't prove their existence. He developed a fascination with small particles, and wrote about them in his *Kinetic Theory of Gases,* which his colleague, Ernst Mach, never tired of mocking. Though Boltzmann tried hard to avoid him, whenever they passed on the street, or even worse attended the same party or official gathering, Mach relished asking him in front of as many people as possible, "Atoms, Ludwig? Have you seen one yet?"

When some people fear they are losing the world as they know it, that losing makes them bitter.

As if this wasn't bad enough, Boltzmann's calculations lead to the idea that within the limits of constraining forces, atoms bounce uncontrollably all over the place. That this is their nature. And because this is reality and not tied to human wishes, Boltzmann found it beautiful. The atoms were blind dancers dancing. He watched and listened. Mostly their language escaped him. It was a music unlike any he had heard, the way the theremin plays itself without human intervention. It was beauty dismantling itself then putting itself back together in a more ruthless, unexpected way, bright paradoxes shining. Rough. Unnerving.

Ernst Mach spent his life studying and photographing shock waves. He loved the material world and found meaning in enhancing its visibility. To the end of his life, he insisted that science and truth must be rooted in sensation. He summarized his ideas in two core principles: 1. Science must be based entirely on observable phenomena. 2. It must completely eschew absolute time and space in favor of relative motion.

Upon his retirement from the University in 1901, Ernst Mach was appointed to the upper chamber of the Austrian Parliament.

Gentleness of lamps at night. Of secret edges. Of the ones who say of animal experiments, The issue is not whether the animals reason or talk but that they suffer. Wild gentleness of the antiparticle, of the queerness of touch, the surveilled, the wandering, the lost, the non-existent. Gentleness that is the transgressor of weight, of gravity. Vagrant gentleness. Radical, insubordinate, unsettled. The body's cells in their most gentle captivity. Basket nests, seeds. Feral gentleness. Gentleness of the torn, the broken. Skeptical, unsweetened.

To Whom It May Concern,

Augustine said his weight was his love and it carried him wherever he needed to be carried. But what I feel is different. It is waves of nothing breaking over waves of nothing.

Maybe now you will see why I cannot return to my current position, and humbly beg you to reassign me to the local library.

Your servant,

Georg Cantor

Funes lay very still. The computer screen glowed blankly. As long as it was empty, it was impossible to know what he was thinking. I chastised myself for being tempted to believe he'd ever let me know him or even know I existed. A lonely sadness washed over me.

When some words appeared, he seemed to be writing about himself, though he started out referring to a man named FM-2030:

The man who re-named himself FM-2030 claimed his aim was to step outside his *encaged historical self.* He said this was a good thing, that his original name was an arbitrary label stamped onto him that he was discarding. And yet he spent his life working for Lockheed and JC Penney, so how was he really setting himself free?

In my case, I can't even remember my life before this white room. All I know is I was hurt, and my legs don't move. I'm unable to forget everything else, but this one thing I can't remember.

Last night I dreamed I was on the moon. Scores of cell towers rose from the lunar surface, surveillance cameras were embedded in the seas and craters. But no matter how close I stood, the surveillance cameras didn't register my presence. I went from one to another, but wherever I moved, their screens stayed empty.

When I woke, I felt those empty screens inside me.

I turned from the blank screen to look at Funes' face, but he was looking toward the far side of the room.

Then I saw in my mind's eye millions of white cubes like Funes', each with its isolate person inside, some of them with a computer, some without, drifting nameless through the starry blackness, their histories unknown or fading. In one cube I saw myself, in another FM-2030.

When I turned back to Funes, he was still turned toward the far distance.

How long had I been drifting through black space? My skin felt hot, did I still have a body?

When Funes' screen went blank, every now and then pieces of my life on Earth came back to me. How several times each week Sister Gudrun took me to the book-lined room she opened with a secret key. We sat side by side by the tall window where she read and I listened. It seemed there was no fact she didn't know, no truth she couldn't find. *The nuclei in a songbird's brain are larger in the spring than in the fall. Honeybees possess the ability to recognize human faces, this is called "configular processing." Spacetime is always changing simply because things happen.*

She said the real is more improbable than the fantastical—more radical, stranger. She stressed this often.

As she read, words opened like moth-wings in the air before me, delicate, intense, confounding. Each syllable shy and brave at the same time.

One day she read about an orphaned boy who stopped growing and nothing in his genes explained this. His parents had died in a war, and from age two he lived in a crowded airplane hangar converted into a makeshift orphanage. All his medical tests came back normal, and no treatment—no vitamin, no medicine, no enzyme—made a difference. Several years passed, a young nurse arrived who took a special liking to the boy. Suddenly he began to grow, and kept growing like a normal boy, and eventually became the subject of an important scientific paper. Whenever the nurse was called away, the boy stopped growing. When she returned, he grew taller.

That night in the darkness, I wondered did she think she was the nurse and I the boy? Was it possible she might come to love me?

But shortly afterwards, her sudden, inexplicable silence began. And then I no longer knew how to stay in the world. I drifted away from humankind.

Only sometimes in the dark, I heard Funes' heartbeat.

Those first, long nights after Sister Gudrun stopped speaking to me, I lay awake waiting for the sound of Funes' heartbeat, hoping I could feel it like before. I still felt closer to him than anyone on Earth, even though I never met him. I pictured him in his room with the barred window, reading and chain-smoking and thinking. How like me, he was alone.

And sometimes, as I stared at the blackened glass of my window, I felt the antiparticles hovering in the air above me, their hurt, mysterious bodies so close and yet I couldn't touch them. I wished they could know what I wished—I wanted them to take me with them. And still I wondered, why did they come so close to Earth? Why did they even want to? From whatever darkness or hiddenness they lived in, did they sense the meager gentleness still left on Earth, and did they want it?

But as night followed night, the air seemed hardly air anymore. It was more like a dream of air on its way to becoming nothing, though I didn't know what nothing was.

And even as I drifted from the Earth, sometimes I still dreamed of Sister Gudrun. Once I saw her standing in a doorway but when I looked again there was only a black cage. It glittered like stars and was cold.

Another time she was standing by the ocean, her eyelids sewn shut with stiff, black stitches.

Funes' screen had been dark for several days. But now the words came back:

In 1984, Hans Dehmelt trapped a positron in a cylinder half the size of a human thumb.

This was the first time antimatter was held captive on Earth.

All the others still roamed free and mysterious as before, traveling at near the speed of light.

Dehmelt named his cylinder a Penning trap. Its walls were magnetic and electric fields. Its vacuum stronger than the moon's, its temperature colder than outer space.

Antihydrogen is bulkier than a positron, and harder to trap. It wasn't captured until 1991. By 2010, it could be held for less than two-tenths of a second.

But in 2011, the ALPHA experiment at CERN trapped cooled antihydrogen for over 16 minutes, long enough for study. The cooling subdues it, makes it less quick.

Antihydrogen is "wild, easily perturbed, erratic." Cooling and imprisonment makes it "well-behaved." Entrapment "promotes de-excitation and manipulates degrees of freedom."

Matter is often called "normal," and antimatter referred to as "matter's evil twin." The familiar is normalized, the unfamiliar made threatening, other.

Imagine trapped antiparticles wildly dancing in their magnetic bottles. Imagine them in free-fall toward their anti-Earth, flying and leaping.

From 1989-2000, 50 meters beneath lawns and vineyards, CERN's Large Electron Positron collider made, contained, and annihilated antimatter.

The positrons sped around a 27-kilometer ring beneath Swiss vineyards at 11,000 times per second, crossed the international border into France, rushed on beneath a statue of Voltaire, then further, under fields, forests, and villages in the Jura mountains.

The Earth's surface appeared completely undisturbed.

In 2000, CERN switched to the more efficient Large Haldron Collider that needs only one bottle of hydrogen gas refilled once or twice per year to create the charged particles that ricochet through it.

CERN also devised an Antimatter Decelerator known as "the best antimatter factory on the planet." A storage ring for antiprotons slowed down enough to study, it is the single place world-wide where antimatter is created daily.

Still, since the discovery of the antiproton in 1955, less than a millionth of a gram of antiprotons have been made on Earth. If this amount annihilated with matter, the energy would be barely enough to light a single electric lightbulb for a few minutes.

These are the verbs commonly found in the experiments: entrap, control, tame, confine, imprison.

But what is matter?

According to the dictionary it is "any substance that has mass and takes up space by having volume." It is what atoms and molecules are made of.

From the Latin *materia*, "hard inner wood of a tree." Also from old French, *materie*, "subject, topic, theme."

Newton listed its qualities as "extension, hardness, impenetrability, mobility, inertia."

But Alfred North Whitehead called it "drops of experience, complex and independent."

He said everything changes from moment to moment. Identity is action, and unstable, a mixture of surprise and opacity. There is flow but no enduring essence.

The reality of brute matter is an illusion.

"Elements which shine with immediate distinctness retire into penumbral shadow, and into black darkness...If we desire the record of uninterpreted experience, we must ask a stone to record its autobiography."

"No entity can be understood apart from how it is interwoven with the rest of the universe."

In lecture halls where other speakers filled hundreds of seats, Whitehead filled few. "About 600 turned up to his first lecture but it was completely unintelligible. My father remarked that if he had not known Whitehead well, he would have suspected he was listening to an imposter making it all up as he went along. At subsequent lectures the audience dwindled to about a half dozen."

The theologian Shailer Mathews remarked, "It is infuriating and I must say embarrassing as well, to read page after page of relatively familiar words and not understand a single sentence."

Still, it is beautiful to think of matter as flux and change, and how each entity exists minute by minute, creating itself over and over. Vulnerable, porous.

How the roots of trees curl and shift, and surfaces touch, and everything living and non-living interacts. No one thing dominates or is the center of power, everything is part of everything else.

Whitehead saw God as a tenderness that moves through the world and cherishes and is changed by the world..."the judgment of a tenderness which loses nothing that can be saved."

"It is as true to say God is permanent and the World fluent, as the World is permanent and God fluent."

"It is as true to say God is one and the World many, as the World is one and God many."

"It is as true to say God creates the world, as the World creates God."

He believed all things possess some measure of creativity and freedom.

"The proper test is not of finality but progress."

"It is the business of the future to be dangerous...the major advances of civilizations all but wreck the societies in which they occur."

His final wish was that his family destroy all his papers.

Dear H,

It appears to me that the "real" is an empty, meaningless category whose monstrous importance lies only in the fact that I can do certain things in it and not certain others. When I was 5, my father showed me a compass. That its needle behaved in a determined way independent of events or direct touch, made a lasting impression on me of something deeply hidden. What we see plainly from infancy and after, causes no similar reaction—we are not surprised over falling bodies or that the moon doesn't fall. Our deepest and most beautiful experiences are of the mysterious.

Yours,

Albert Einstein

The Most Expensive Substances in the World by Weight

Saffron: $26 per gram.

Platinum: $27 per gram.

Beluga caviar: $37 per gram.

Gold: $38 per gram.

Heroin: $125 per gram.

Gold powder: $125 per gram.

Spider venom: $1,225 per gram.

Plutonium: $3,679 per gram.

Soliris: $20,850 per gram.

Tritium: $27,800 per gram.

Diamonds: $55,000 per gram.

Californium: $24,530,000 per gram.

Antimatter: $22,000,000,000 per gram.

Why had those substances appeared to Funes? What did they mean to him?

Even Whitehead, who, unlike Funes, had been able to live in the world, said the reality of brute matter is an illusion.

As I drifted through the darkness, I felt more like Whitehead's drops of experience than anything knowable or stable, anything that could be touched or even described. I was a sentence undoing itself in the dark. I was waves and I was dissolving. I was Funes' friend who never met him. I was with him, and I was alone.

Often when the black sadness overcame me, I had only to remember how out of one small point of unimaginable density, energy burst forth at a speed of 300,000,000 meters per second in every direction and the universe came into being. It soothed me to contemplate how after another billion years, the first galaxies began, and the antiparticles took shelter in their secret darkness. But now that I am dead and shift back and forth in time, often in the first seconds after waking I feel the walls of the vacuum trap, the steel tunnels of the collider blowing me apart.

Your servant,

Ludwig Boltzmann

I had been drifting through the darkness a long time. The moon was very near now, exposed and soundless, oddly fragile. The air had grown colder. All around me, pieces of fragmentation debris moved in orbital precision—motor casings, fly wheels, lens caps, needles. Detritus of the human world. Stray gloves and barcodes. Zone after zone of damaged freedom. Waves of light like silver foil shivered on my skin. Then I saw the vague footprints on the lunar surface that with no weather to erode them will remain for billions of years, maybe until the moon's extinction. Quiet, unchanging. The entire lunar surface becalmed and injured. In a way it was like Funes—immobile, trapped within a harsh exposure.

Waves of radiation from colliding stellar corpses penetrated the lunar rocks like soft tissue.

I drifted further from the sun, the dark grew darker. Was Funes drifting with me too?

The moon was a black void among the stars.

Was it possible Funes was also near the moon? I knew I couldn't know, but when these words came on his screen I wondered even more:

On March 18, 1965, Alexi Leonov became the first human to walk in space.

Before exiting the capsule of Vokshod 2, he slipped a cyanide pill into his spacesuit pocket. After all, no one had ever walked in space, it was impossible to predict what might happen.

Later he described it, "Attached to the end of the rope, I swam smoothly in one direction, then another. The silence was so vast and deep I heard my muscles and blood vessels stretch and contract. The whole sky was a fathomless deep black and at the same time bright with sunlight. From the quiet of my heart, I sent greetings to the lilies of the valley. In the vastness of space, the only moving thing I saw was the Earth revolving."

But when his co-pilot told him to return to the capsule, his spacesuit was so grossly bloated from the lack of atmospheric pressure, he couldn't fit through the airlock. No one was prepared for this. In desperation, he released the suit's stored oxygen through its valve, and pushed clumsily back inside. "Almost no one knew how close I came to being stranded in outer space. Luckily, the televised part of the mission was over."

Four years later, the three crew members of Apollo 11 headed for the moon with miniature headsets taped to their ears as Houston fed them baseball scores, stock market quotes, instructions on camera angles and the adjustments of their biomedical sensors.

On July 20, 1969, while Neil Armstrong and Buzz Aldrin walked on the moon, their co-pilot Michael Collins orbited alone. No one had ever been alone on the moon's far side. Out of signal range, even Houston couldn't reach him. Later, when asked if he felt profoundly alone, he said he'd felt peaceful. His only worry was if the retrieval of the moon-lander didn't work, Armstrong and Aldrin would be left on the moon and he would be forced to return to Earth without them. For years afterward, this nightmare still woke him.

But as he orbited the moon, "The noisy arguments of the Earth were silenced. Orange dust clouds from the Sahara drifted over the Philippines, there were no human boundaries."

He carried a small white fiberglass satchel filled with four packs of chewing gum and a hollowed-out seed containing fifty delicately carved ivory elephants the size of fingernail clippings.

Alone, he orbited for 21 hours.

Years later he described the moon. "Up close, it looks like a withered, sun-seared peach pit... mysterious and subtle, but there is no comfort in it." And the astronaut Jim Lovell, from a later mission, called it "a vast loneliness...gray...like dirty beach sand or plaster of Paris. Uninteresting... battered, ugly."

Neil Armstrong said that seeing it up close was "like the difference between watching a real football game and watching it on TV."

And Alan Shepard remarked, "When I play golf, I can hit farther on the moon, but my swing is better on Earth."

Mostly the astronauts spoke less about the moon than the Earth, how vulnerable and endangered it seemed, and small like a blue marble, how innocent in the vastness of space.

Years later Michael Collins said very quietly, "I want no part in destroying."

Rogue planets are also known as orphan planets. Violently ejected from their orbits, they wander the galaxy alone without sunrise or sunset, in darkness and in cold. There is no parent star to light or warm them.

They are so lightless it is impossible for the naked human eye to find them.

The physicist Takahiro Sumi estimates there are as many as 400 billion in the Milky Way alone. He says it is even likely the majority of planets are orphaned, it's just that we can't see them.

Through the use of gravitational microlensing, he and his team in Osaka, Japan, have located ten, each around the size of Jupiter. Gravitational microlensing measures the changes in a star's brightness when a planet passes in front of it. In this way alone it is possible to find lightless planets. Knowledge comes through indirection.

"By measuring the duration of a microlensing event and the shape of its light curve, we can estimate the mass of the unseen object."

In September 2020, a new rogue planet, OGLE-2016-BLG-1928, was discovered by astronomers in Chile, its frozen, lightless body somewhere between the size of Earth and Mars.

The birth of a planet is violent and erratic. Takiro Sumi says catastrophic events and unforeseen collisions remain a constant danger. One sudden, random act can thrust a planet from its orbit. Once ejected, it is impossible to get back in.

He says although we see billions of stars in the night sky, there are at least as many starless planets wandering among them. But they are unreal to us because we do not see them.

Arthur Schopenhauer said, "Every man takes the limits of his own field of vision for the limits of the world."

And Stephen Gould pointed out, "Facts are not pure, unsullied bits of information."

Kahlil Gibran wrote: "How narrow is the vision that exalts the busyness of the ant above the singing of the grasshopper."

Still, it is hard to *feel* the presence of the wandering, unseen planets. The presence of the real, the actual. All the fraught, unstable migrations, isolation. Cell changes in a living body. Dark planets.

"The history of astronomy is a history of receding horizons."

In *The Problem of the Expanding Universe*, Edward Hubble revealed that contrary to accepted thought, the universe is not one galaxy, but many. What were believed to be nebulae—clouds of gas and dust—are in fact other galaxies. The idea of centrality took one more blow.

"Here is the letter that destroyed my universe," the physicist Harlow Shapley lamented to his friend, as he clutched Hubble's letter explaining his discovery. Where there was unity, there is multiplicity, where there was wholeness, there is fracture and difference.

Where once there was one kind of beauty, there is now another kind of beauty that needs new eyes to see it.

Using the largest telescope of his time, Hubble discovered the faster a galaxy appears to be receding, the greater its distance from Earth. He calculated galaxies move away at a velocity of 90 miles per second for every light year of increasing distance. The space between celestial bodies grows ever emptier, vaster. Time brings increasing isolation.

Like Ernst Mach before him, he privileged direct observation. Theory is *dreamy speculation*: "Not until the empirical resources are exhausted, need we pass on to the realm of dreamy speculation."

"Equipped with our five senses, we explore the universe around us and call the adventure Science."

And yet, "Eventually we reach the utmost limits of our telescopes, the dim boundary. There, we measure shadows, and search among ghostly errors."

He discovered the Andromeda Nebula, created a classification system for galaxies, measured distances and velocities in deep space, used the *Cepheid variable* as a guide, scrutinized the red shifts of stars.

Einstein thanked him for his findings, which supported his theories.

In the first world war he fought in France, in the second he developed weapon technology.

His name has been given to a telescope, a moon crater, an asteroid.

At the age of 63, in San Marino California, he died of a cerebral hemorrhage.

Faithful to her husband's wishes, his wife declined to reveal where he is buried.

Interviewer: Can you put into layman's terms what you're working on, Professor?

Paul Dirac: Yes. Creation.

Interviewer: That sounds very interesting. Can you say more?

Paul Dirac: Creation was one vast bang.

Interviewer: But if nothing existed beforehand what was there to bang?

Paul Dirac: That is not a meaningful question.

Interviewer: Can you explain what electrons and protons are?

Paul Dirac: To ask what they are is not profitable and does not really have a meaning. The important thing about electrons and protons is not what they are but how they behave.

Freeman Dyson: Well, Professor Dirac, what do you think of these new developments in quantum electrodynamics?

Paul Dirac: I might have thought the new ideas were correct if they had not been so ugly.

The moon was behind me now, a small clot of shadowed brightness.

Anaxagorus said in everything there is a portion of everything else, there is no such thing as isolation. And Whitehead said everything exists in relation to everything else. But now, as I drifted further, I wondered, even though I could read the words on Funes' screen, wasn't our connection a tensile, fragile thread that could break at any moment? That maybe loneliness was the truest thing about us. In a split-second I could lose him.

Though time felt almost immeasurable to me now, a gap of time arrived when Funes and his screen were suddenly nowhere in sight. I saw only blackness.

Like the antiparticles, it seemed he had simply vanished.

I felt a loneliness like the first days of Sister Gudrun's silence.

Sherlock Holmes said to Watson, "When you have eliminated the impossible, whatever remains, however improbable, must be the truth." But how could I eliminate the impossible? How could I know what it was? Once I was sure I'd felt Funes' heartbeat. But after that, I didn't know where he was or where I was. And now I couldn't find him at all. Holmes listened to objects, turned words inside out, said his business was to know what other people wanted to know but couldn't. Where Watson saw an inviting house, Holmes saw a potential crime scene. No object was too small for contemplation.

But adrift in darkness, what could I investigate, what tell-tale objects could I find? What hints out of the voids between the stars and planets?

I heard the footprints on the moon softly crying.

I told myself I would never see him again. That whatever he was to me had vanished into loss and silence. That this is what the universe is—vast, without pity.

But then suddenly he reappared. His glowing screen had filled with thicker shapes than before.

I realized he was watching a movie. Its title was *X Men*. Aside from a few short clips, I'd never seen him watch anything. But now, as I thought about it, it was strange he hadn't. As with most everything, I had no explanation.

As before, I could see but couldn't hear. I tried reading lips, but most of what was said went past me. I knew there were events and causes, but didn't know what they were. Feelings leapt from face to face, ideas like errant winds inside them. Funes' watching face stayed largely impassive, though once he smiled, and once his eyes brimmed with tears. He paused and replayed that scene several times. What could be be thinking?

In the scene, Professor X was in his wheelchair in a book-lined office. Bald, well dressed in an expensive tailored suit, and with a strong, chiseled face, he conveyed an air of worldliness. He was talking to a distraught younger man in a gray sweatshirt. His expression seemed firm but also kind.

The camera zoomed in further and I read his lips.

You have wandered alone for 15 years, living from day to day, from place to place, with no memory of who or what you are. You are weary beyond measure. I give you my word, I will use all my powers to help you piece together what you have lost.

Maybe now I could begin to understand Funes' tears. Wasn't he watching two halves of himself—the one with extreme mental powers who can't walk, and the other who is lost and can't remember who he is. Though unlike the Professor's promise, Funes was unable to piece together the life he lost and couldn't remember.

Then suddenly the screen went dark.

Whatever Funes was thinking, there was no way I could know it.

The screen was lit again, and the silent shapes moved across it.

Professor X wheeled himself through a metallic, silver tunnel and into an enormous vault-like room with spherical silver walls. The heavy, motorized door slid shut behind him. It was like being inside a spaceship, but larger, less narrow. The Professor secured his wheelchair at a workstation on a gleaming silver plank overlooking the cavernous distance below.

He placed a device like a metal helmet on his head. It seemed to interface with the surrounding walls.

The walls flared with a convulsive, violent light. Everything reeling and still at the same time. Ghostly figures rose through clumps of fog, solidified into people on a street, defined and moving through their daily lives. Body after body, face after face.

It was like watching a dream of something true, but you can't understand what it is.

Funes' skin was the color of dried paste. I had no idea what he was thinking.

A document was up on Funes' screen—at first, I couldn't tell what it was. Then I realized it was a short biographical article about Professor X.

It said he was born Charles Francis Xavier into a wealthy New York family (his father was a nuclear scientist) and lost both parents early—his father to a mysterious accident; his mother of a general decline a few years later. As a child, he realized he possessed telepathic powers, and gradually came to understand he was a member of a gifted and oppressed mutant off-shoot of the human race. He earned 4 PhD's by his mid-twenties, later an MD in psychiatry.

After serving in the Korean war and traveling the world, he made a vow to devote his life to safeguarding the innocent and fighting human oppression. In the Himalayas, his legs were crushed by a stone block—this left him permanently crippled. (Is this what first drew Funes' attention to him?)

Nevertheless he went on to make his name as a distinguished geneticist and psychologist who founded a school for young mutants, and, although insisting on his pacifist inclinations, convened his own small band of mutant soldiers.

He invented a device, Cerebro, which could magnify the brainwaves and enhance the psychic powers of its user. To use it demanded great discipline, as the increased psychic input was easily overwhelming and could result in insanity, brain damage, coma, even death. (I realized that was what I saw in the movie.)

Professor X's telepathic powers gave him access to the thoughts of others and often he could project his thoughts into their brains. He mastered foreign languages by accessing their language centers. He communicated with animals and shared their perceptions. When invisibility proved useful, he manipulated others to be unable to see him. He induced in his targets limited or total amnesia. In almost no time whatsoever, he could assimilate huge amounts of raw data. Over the years, he broke and rebuilt countless minds.

Unlike Funes, his legs were briefly healed and he could walk.

I wondered what Funes would think of him using his powers to break others' minds. And of how, unlike Funes, he was rarely ever alone.

He died many times and many times came back to life.

If not for Funes, would my years on Earth seem little more than a dream to me by now? But the tears in his eyes, his injured legs, the way he kept trying to figure things out, were like a rope pulling me back—like the rope attaching Leonov to the spaceship capsule.

You are weary beyond measure, Professor X said to the young man in the gray sweatshirt. Is that how Funes also felt, even as he pursued his investigations?

He seemed weaker now, his legs more withered, his worn face pallid, chiseled.

If you know a particle's velocity and momentum you can't know its position.

If you know its position, you can't know its velocity and momentum.

"It was around three o'clock in the morning when the final results of my calculations were before me. At first, I was profoundly alarmed. I had the feeling I had gone beyond the surface of things and felt dizzy...I left the house and began walking slowly in the dark. I climbed a rock overlooking the sea to the tip of the island and waited for the sunrise to come up..." Werner Heisenberg wrote this at the age of 23. In his desire to let go of his received ideas of the real, he had isolated himself on the island of Helgoland.

"The electron no longer has a trajectory." There is probability but not prediction.

"What we call reality is a vast web of interacting entities. Quantum theory is the theory of how things influence each other. The human observer is a part of the interaction, nothing in existence stands outside it."

In his memoirs Heisenberg is often walking, and often he talks with a companion as they walk. "Science is a conversation."

Year after year he walks on the hills and mountains of Germany and Switzerland, over snow fields and fields of flowers. He walks above the western shore of Lake Starnberg, "It was here I had my first conversation about the world of atoms...in the confusion of the times, we had discovered a new sense of freedom." He stuffs a manuscript in a rucksack and sets out from Gudbrandsdal across several mountain chains to Sogne Fjord. He walks with Niels Bohr in a park in Copenhagen. With Wolfgang Pauli he bicycles up the steep western shore of Lake Walchen, confiding how he grasps Einstein's theory with his brain but not yet with his heart.

He expresses gratitude to the agitated black dog that yapped at him with undisguised animosity during an interview, ruining his chances of being accepted as a student by the dog's owner, the mathematician Ferdinand von Lindemann, who had no patience for physics.

Throughout his life, he is consoled by music: "A young violinist appeared on the balcony above the courtyard. He struck up the first great D minor chords of Bach's Chaconne. All at once, and with utter certainty, I had found my link with the center." And toward the end of his life, "Von Holst fetched his violin...Beethoven's D Major Serenade brimmed over with vital force and joy, and as I listened, I grew less weary...life and science would always go on..."

Nothing is truly known or certain, everything must be called into question.

What does it even mean "to observe?"

"No wonder Mach's principle has such a suspiciously commercial name: *thought economy*. He pretends we know perfectly well what 'observe' means, and thinks this exempts him from having to discriminate between 'objective' and 'subjective' phenomena."

"We have no idea in what language we must speak. We are ignorant even of this."

To the end, he comforted himself with the words of Niels Bohr, "The opposite of a correct statement is a false statement. But the opposite of a profound truth may well be another profound truth."

In 1915 Karl Schwarzschild devised the exact solution to Einstein's field equations of general relativity while serving as a soldier on the Russian Front. The equations had only been revealed a few weeks before, and Einstein had been unable to come up with the exact formulation.

"As you see, the war has treated me kindly enough, in spite of heavy gunfire, to allow me to get away from it all and take a walk in the land of your ideas," Schwarzschild wrote to Einstein in a letter dated December 22, 1915.

His solution led him to the theoretical basis for black holes. Though his calculations were undeniably sound, the idea of black holes was considered so bizarre it was beyond acceptable, and almost no one, including Schwarzschild, believed they existed.

Nevertheless, he proved that bodies of sufficient mass possess an escape velocity exceeding the speed of light, and therefore are not available to direct observation. That when mass is compressed to an extreme extent, it undergoes an irreversible gravitational collapse—no known force or pressure can stop it. The inevitable result is a black hole.

Even before he sent his letter to Einstein, Schwarzschild was manifesting the early symptoms of the rare, debilitating illness of the skin that would kill him a year later at the age of 42. Some believed the illness was brought on by repeated exposure to poison gases in the trenches.

At the time of his enlistment the year before, he was Director of the Astrophysical Observatory in Potsdam, the most prestigious post for an astronomer in Germany.

As a child, with money he saved from his allowance, he built a telescope and showed his six brothers and sisters the rings of Saturn. When given piano lessons, he displayed little interest in the music itself but was fascinated by the mechanics of the piano, the creation and theory of sound vibrations.

Throughout his school years, he carried a notebook wherever he went, including on hiking trips to the Harz mountains.

By age 16, he published two scientific papers on the orbital determination of planets and double stars. His younger brother recalled, "The whole family was very proud and we read the papers several times, but none of us understood a single word."

He believed all fields inform each other. His mature research ranged over celestial mechanics, stellar structure, spectroscopy, photometry, and quantum mechanics.

He wrote, "It is more important to lift a veil than to stand back and look upon it with respectful awe."

In 1905 he journeyed to Algiers for the sole purpose of observing the total solar eclipse.

He developed an instrument that yielded the color-index of stars.

For his obituary in the Astrophysical Journal Volume XLV Number 3 June 1917, the Danish astronomer, Ejnar Hertzsprung, wrote, "If he had known beforehand that his life would be so short, he could not have used it to a better purpose... In his work, many pearls are hidden where we would not naturally think to look for them. Data alone never satisfied him, he gave us observations that lead to new thoughts, new methods."

Hertzsprung recalled their final meeting. "Even on his deathbed, the ardent wish for scientific occupation never left him. Though his body was weak, he possessed the mastery of strong spirit over earthly misery."

Schwarzschild wrote, "Theoretical mastery is the highest step on the ladder of the human mind."

And: "I like to be contradicted."

Several decades after his father's death, at the age of 30, his youngest son was murdered by the Nazis.

I must enter the Cloud of the Impossible, Nicholas Cusanus wrote in the 15c.

To be *kindled by wonder we must lift the eyes of the mind.*

As in: the Earth is not superior to other planetary bodies. "It may be conjectured that in the area of the sun there exist solar beings, bright and enlightened denizens whose nature is more spiritual than those as may inhabit the moon, and less gross and material than those of us on Earth."

"Rather than think this Earth of ours alone is peopled, we can suppose that in every region of the stars and heavens there are inhabitants who are beyond our knowledge and judgment; we possess no standards by which to appraise them."

The natural universe is comprised of "as many diverse areas as there are uncountable stars." It has no center, its circumference is everywhere and nowhere.

He said the only knowledge we can have is that the absolute truth, such as it is, is beyond human reach. He called this *learned ignorance.* To be knowledgeable is to know you cannot know.

"In God absolute unity is multiplicity, absolute identity is absolute diversity, absolute actuality is absolute potentiality."

Reason is like an eye that looks at a face from different positions. Each view is true, but partial.

This realization came to him in a vision on a sea voyage home from Constantinople in 1437.

His treatises include: *On Learned Ignorance, On Conjecture, The Layman: About Mind, On the Not Other, Experiments with Weights.*

He said, "All things exist in the best way they are able to exist."

When he died his body was buried in Rome in the Church of St. Peter in Chains, though later lost.

His heart was sent to the hospital chapel in the town of Kues, where he was born.

In his will he endowed a hospice to house thirty-three indigent, elderly men, in honor of the thirty-three years of Christ's earthly life. It still stands today, and serves its original purpose.

As the words disappeared and reappeared on Funes' screen, I kept wondering, if Nikolas Cusanus is right, and all things exist in the best way they are able to exist, why is Funes paralyzed, why are the facts of the world trapped inside his immobilized body? Why are human minds built of hiddenness and darkness, with barely a speck of what's inside able to reach the outside world? And why must Tsiolkovsky's atoms be tormented? Why must galaxies pull increasingly away? Why do poison gases sweep across fields and settle in lungs that can't expel them?

The shy accidents of my cells had grown tenuous and thinning. My chains of questions trembled in the fever-light of stars.

Dear S,

Often I have been unfaithful to the heavens. My interest has never been limited to the things beyond the moon, but has followed the threads from the outermost reaches into our deepest, unknown selves. But now something is happening inside me that has an irrepressible force and is nameless and darkens all my thoughts. It is a shadow, void without form or dimension, yet I feel it with all my soul. When the poison gases swept across the fields, the moon crossed the sky with such quickness time itself sped up. This phenomenon was so strange and unsettling it seemed a bad omen. I remember another time as well, the moon's shadow rushing toward me over the hills at Algiers, and then the moon covered the sun—from behind it, a corona of frail light fanned out.

Yours faithfully,

Karl Schwarzschild

Dark matter holds the universe together. Without it, the Milky Way would tear itself apart.

There is approximately 24 trillion metric tons between the Earth and moon. But because it does not interact, we cannot see or touch it. It is its nature to elude direct proof.

What we can see and feel is next to nothing of what is.

In 1884, Lord Kelvin estimated the mass of the Milky Way as different from the mass of its visible stars. In 1906, Henri Poincare named that invisible difference *matière obscure*, dark matter. In 1933, Fritz Zwicky estimated the Coma Cluster, a cluster of galaxies, possesses 400 times more mass than is visibly observable. Because the amount of luminous matter is insufficient to enable the rotation curves clearly observed, it must be the presence of dark matter that accounts for the rapid speed of their orbits.

You don't feel it, but it holds the globe, the universe, together. At this moment it is touching your hand. It is deep in the hearts of stars.

It is cold, collisionless, and we do not know it.

There are many theories but no certainty. (Nikolas Cusanus said we live in Learned Ignorance.)

One study used slime mold simulations to map the way dark matter holds the universe together. Joseph Burchett, the lead researcher said, "It is fascinating that one of the simplest forms of life enables insight into the universe's very largest."

"There is a striking similarity between how the slime mold builds complex filaments to capture new food, and how gravity constructs the cosmic web strands between galaxies and clusters of galaxies."

"The algorithm gave us a picture of dark matter."

In 2020, the Hubble telescope detected the smallest known clumps of dark matter. "It is even colder than we knew."

And in 2018, the Hubble's Advanced Camera for Surveys detected a galaxy seemingly devoid of dark matter. NGC 1052-DF2 is known as a "see-through galaxy,"—its stars are thinly spread out. Almost as wide as the Milky Way, it possesses no dense central region and contains only 1/200th the number of its stars. But if dark matter holds everything together, how can this galaxy exist without it?

In another strange case, scientists think the "ghostly galaxy", NGC 1052 DF4, was stripped of its dark matter when another galaxy's tidal forces swept it away. Now isolate in space, it drifts far from any cluster.

I remember Stephen Gould said, "Facts are not pure, unsullied bits of information." And Nikolas Cusanus said, all we can know is that we do not know.

Why should the real be visible? Why do we place so much trust in our eyes? Why do we doubt what exists but we can't see it?

William Blake said, *If the sun and moon should doubt they'd immediately go out.*

An article published in the *Astrophysical Journal* in 2021, says according to an international team of scientists, recent observations suggest dark matter may not exist, but is instead the result of our incomplete understanding of gravity. They say they have evidence to show this.

The astrophysicist Priyamvada Natarajan says, "I find the world with its inequities and injustices to be messy, unfair, and complicated. The cosmos, on the other hand, is orderly and beautiful—this I find captivating and alluring."

Once again, for a long time I couldn't see Funes at all. I kept searching for some glimmer of computer light, the faintest ember from a cigarette.

He had seemed even paler, weaker. I worried he was failing.

Thoughts ride on secret waves from one body to another, one mind to another, but those waves had vanished.

Can meaning wound and destroy itself? It seemed that's what it was doing.

If everything in the universe is moving away from everything else, were Funes and I also moving away from each other? Why should we be different from the stars and planets?

I was afraid I had lost him.

And then like before he was back again, so sudden. But I still saw how worn he looked and thin, I didn't trust what I was seeing. As if a flame was slowly dying.

Still, I was relieved to see the lit screen, to know what he was reading:

Excerpts from A Talk by Elon Musk (Chief Executive Officer, Space X), *Making Humans a Multi-Planetary Species, September 2016*

"One path is we stay on Earth forever. The alternative is to become a space-faring civilization and multi-planetary species, which I hope you agree is the right way to go.

Some people wonder, why Mars? Our options of becoming a multi-planetary species are limited. Venus is a super-high pressure hot acid bath. Mercury is way too close to the sun. We could conceivably go to our moon, and I actually have nothing against our moon, but it is much too small, and it has no atmosphere.

Mars is far better-suited to scale up to be a self-sustaining civilization. It is a little cold, but we can warm it up.

The early Mars was a lot like Earth. When we warm it up, it will have liquid oceans again, and it has decent sunlight. Its atmosphere is primarily CO2 which means we can grow plants just by compressing the atmosphere.

It would be quite fun to be on Mars because you would have gravity that is about 37% that of Earth, so you would could lift heavy things and bound around.

We just need to change the populations, currently we have seven billion people on Earth and none on Mars.

So we will need to build a city.

If we can get the cost of moving to Mars roughly equivalent to a median house price in the United States, which is around $200,000, then I think the probability of establishing a self-sustaining civilization is very high. I think it would almost certainly occur.

Not everyone would want to go.

Almost anyone, if they saved up and this was their goal, could buy a ticket and move to Mars. There would be a lot of job openings.

Generally, I do not like calling things 'systems', as everything is a system, including your dog. However, for interplanetary travel beyond Mars, there would be a system consisting of four components that would give you the freedom to go anywhere. You could travel out to the Kuiper Belt, to the Oort cloud. I would not recommend it for interstellar journeys, but for within the solar system it would be fine."

There are 5,157 known exoplanets in 3,800 planetary systems.

Proxima Centauri b is the closest to Earth, approximately 4 light years away.

On HD-189773b the rain is made of glass. Its winds gust up to 4,000 miles per hour.

Kelt19b burns so intensely it rips its own molecules apart.

The surface of Kepler51b is the texture of cotton candy.

Gliese-436b is covered with burning ice and ten different solid states of water.

On PSR B1257-12 pulsing light-beams sweep over its entire surface, its sky lashed with tendrils of light.

J14077b has 640 times as many rings as Saturn.

Beta Pictorus b orbits in a disc of debris.

Gliese581 is "tidally locked"—one side always faces its star.

On TrES-2b, 99% of the gas that reaches it is immediately absorbed. It looks like a black sphere of burning gas.

There are no land-forms on Gj12149. Its surface is entirely covered in water.

Hat-P-7b is subject to violent storms. Its rain is made of sapphires and rubies.

According to Werner Heisenberg, the universe is not only stranger than we think, it is stranger than we can think. What we can say of its almost frightening simplicity amounts to almost nothing. It's not nature we observe, but nature exposed to our method of questioning.

He said we must learn a new meaning of the word 'understanding'.

I thought of Funes and myself, that whatever understanding is, which has to do with *having a clear and complete idea of* and *perceiving the intended meaning*—it seemed as far away as Earth. Even that time I felt his heartbeat, how could I really know who he was? I looked again at his sallow cheek, his withered legs. A deepening sadness came over me.

I understood he was growing even weaker.

I remembered his heartbeat. How it felt like a small animal, exposed and unprotected.

The dark was growing vaster. Glowing dust and ice-specks swept across my hair and lips, a mute violence inside them. Secret histories I'd never know. Had I passed the rings of Saturn? Was even the Earth's sun behind me? I drifted further.

The memory of Funes' heartbeat felt like a leaden weight inside me. I fell into a restless sleep. Funes was on Earth again, lying in a sunlit garden among stone paths and flowers. His wrists were strong again, his skin less pallid. A black fly alighted on his cheek. I wondered why he didn't swat it away. Then I saw it wasn't a fly but the letter a, and the longer I looked, the more letters alighted, until his face was a black void among the starry flowers. After a while, Ludwig Boltzmann appeared beside him. I could hear him speaking. *Once I, too, became the dark side of the moon. It was the night after Mardi Gras, everyone was dancing and singing, but wherever I stepped there were strange patches of dead quiet. I realized these patches were the antiparticles looking down in longing at the Earth. The more I listened, gravity weakened around me and then I wasn't on Earth anymore, but I wasn't among the antiparticles either. I was a black void among the stars and I was alone. Sometimes even now I still hear the ocean at Duino, its rough singing.*

The number of carbon atoms in one inkdot on paper is greater than the sum of all humans who ever existed.

The mass of a black hole the size of a pinprick is greater than the mass of Earth's tallest mountain.

Time passes faster in the mountains than at the sea.

A clock on the floor runs a little more slowly than a clock on the table.

The more humankind learns about time, the more our notions of time disintegrate.

In the 13th century, Robert Grosseteste said our world-machine is corruptible, various, imperfect. He said light is the form and perfection of all bodies.

A map is a set of agreed-upon errors.

The words on the screen had grown smoke-like, fragile. They seemed almost to crumble:

Large stars are violent, but smaller stars meet in *soft collisions.*

I must ask myself what and is. I must learn so much more about and.

Since Einstein's theory, our world is much harder to live in, less certain, more lonely.

The screen was often dark now. Mostly I was alone in darkness.

Every now and then the flickering strip of screen came back:

Can we imagine a vast expanse without motion or mass where atom and anti-atom unite?

Surely something is missing in our conception of the universe. Let us dream then of a world.

Arthur Schuster, August 18, 1898

What, then, are *things*? A chair, a sail, an eye, what are they? If things are forms of forms of forms and if forms are order...

When you disturb the smallest petal of a flower, you trouble the most distant star.

On the glowing strip of screen the letters seemed to crumble even further. Much blackness came, and then:

I am a speck of stellar matter that got cold by accident, a blown fragment of a star gone wrong.

Those were the last words I ever saw on Funes' screen. I never saw him or the screen again.

Did he see himself as a blown fragment of a star gone wrong? It hurt me to think this.

I wished I could go to him, that he knew I'd watched him. I didn't know if he was even still alive.

Inside my mind, I lay down on his cot that smelled of lit matches, cigarettes. I held his heartbeat close to mine.

After a while, I opened my eyes. My heart beat loudly in my chest. I turned back to the blackness and the stars.

My skin was blackness and silence.

Einstein said the universe loves simplicity and beauty. Sister Gudrun told me he believed this to the very end.

I didn't know.

Soft, black waves pressed against my skin. I was afraid that even they would leave me.

...If only I could feel Funes' heartbeat...

My skin was black whispers. A wind like shattered glass moved through me.

Maybe there never was a narrow cot or a lit screen or Michael Collins or Professor X.

Maybe I never felt Funes' heartbeat next to mine or saw the words appear on the lit screen.

Kant said reason is monstrous that doesn't know itself in time, but I couldn't know if time died or what it is or if I was even in it anymore.

I remembered how Funes' screen said we must learn a new meaning of the word 'understanding'.

Every now and then some words came back to me:

...........If you know a particle's velocity and momentum you can't know its position...........The least particle is full of an infinity of different creatures...........

...........Maybe there never were any stars, any planets...........Maybe none of it existed...........

Nothing is more difficult than emptiness...........Atoms, Ludwig, have you seen one yet?...........I must ask myself what *and* is...........

...........When you disturb the smallest petal you trouble the most distant star...........But if there are no stars, no petals...........I couldn't feel the black waves anymore...........Maybe there never was a black dress, a white screen, a heartbeat...........

2. Sagittarius A*

The black hole Sagittarius A* lies at the very center of the Milky Way, 25,640 light years from Earth. Made of pure gravity, it is thirty times more massive than the sun, and nothing, not even light, can escape.

I stood on the Event Horizon, confused and dizzy.

To my left, three arms of spiraling red light moved in a silent ballet. Dust clouds swept from one swathe of blackness to another, powerful winds pushed a comet-tail around a giant blue star. Farther off, bolts of frozen lightning flashed among milky wisps of crystalized carbon, clouds of nitrogen ice, silicon, ethyl formate.

I never knew that blackness could be so chaotic.

How could I have gotten here? How could this have happened?

Sometimes the dust grew so thick I couldn't see.

I had no words for what seemed a kind of peaceful violence or violent peace. Light and wind almost the same thing.

How could I even be intact here? I should have been immediately swallowed and crushed.

The air was loud but a vast silence spread inside it.

Red waves swept across my face.

What if I remained here forever? What if all that remained were these red waves and the black hole and silence?

What if this is what entropy is.

A jagged fear moved through me.

Then suddenly I heard a rustling sound that reminded me of something on Earth but I couldn't think of what. Maybe the sound of breath or moving cloth. It came from a far distance. I looked around but the dust clouds made it hard to see.

When finally the dust cleared I saw a black hole in the distance. On top was a black speck. I realized it was Sister Gudrun.

She spoke across the blackness.

Did you think you were the only one out here, she said. *Did you really believe only you would come this far?* Her voice was meaured, calm.

Of course I know you would like me to step across the Event Horizon and disappear forever. You believe that then you would be free.

But do you really think my disappearance would make any difference? You'd still want to know why I stopped speaking to you. Just look at the facts- all this time you haven't been able to stop wondering, even though you've traveled far from Earth. Always you go over and over it in your mind, even when you think you aren't: how could she have done this to me, why would she suddenly shun me like that? Why was she so cruel? You have grown tired of my black clothes, my silence, how even in black space you see me walking in the courtyard. My turned back. My heavy shoes. How you and I exist like Saturn's rings, circling, never touching.

You believe I have left you in the dark forever.

You want me to give an explanation but I never will.

The air is very cold here. Always it is like this now. Even my clothes are black ice, my mind burning with black ice.

Maybe you also feel this where you are.

At first I thought I was dreaming, or the black hole was playing tricks on me. But after some time, her voice continued.

It wasn't hard to predict you would end up here, though of course you didn't realize it yourself.

You understand you are on the Event Horizon of Sagittarius A but what do you really know of where you are? You lack perspective. You always have. It is one reason you are far from Earth.*

Even now, you stand only in one place, you look out from the same spot, the same angle. But seeing can't happen from one angle only.

Consider the physicist Karl Jansky who discovered your black hole in 1931. He knew how to investigate and question, to not get stuck in one angle or assumption.

Hired by Bell Labs to track down the source of static interference on its phone lines, he grew puzzled that his antenna was picking up a faint steady hiss, and more than that, the hiss repeated on a cycle of 23 hours and 56 minutes, the exact period of the Earth's rotation relative to the stars. After extensive calculations, he realized the hum must be emanating from the constellation Sagittarius. This was the first known sign of Sagittarius A. But when he brought his astonishing finding to Bell Labs they said they couldn't justify the cost of pursuing it further as it had no bearing on trans-Atlantic communication. They re-assigned him to another project.*

It wasn't until 1982 that your black hole was finally named by the astronomer Robert Brown who explained he included the asterisk because he found the black hole exciting and the asterisk denotes the excited state of atoms. Many think it's pronounced Sagittarius A asterisk, but in fact the correct pronunciation is Sagittarius A star.

In a time of lies it survives as something true. The pure embodiment of chaos.

But what have you accomplished by going to such a place? You have abandoned the Earth as once, as an infant, you were abandoned.

Do you really think that is a good thing?

But now I have said more than enough. I can't tolerate much time outside my silence.

How had she found me? How could she even know where I was? Why would she bother?

I had been sure I would never hear her voice again. Never see her.

Whitehead called matter a mixture of surprise and opacity. I remembered seeing that on Funes' screen. And now, looking at the black smudge in the distance, that smudge I now knew was Sister Gudrun, I felt that's what I was seeing.

But she had finished speaking, so why was she still there? Why hadn't she left me?

Once again she was speaking:

You believe my silence hurled you from the world. That I was cruel to stop speaking to you. But think of all the books we read, all the hours we shared by the tall window. For a while you almost convinced yourself I loved you.

You were so little when I first started reading to you. I sat you in a chair by the window and read you things you couldn't possibly understand. I told myself you would take from them what you could, they would give you what you needed. Things I could never predict or even imagine. All along I believed this. I can still almost feel it in my hands, all those hours turning pages. Of course you never dreamed I would stop speaking to you. Never dreamed I would refuse to look into your face or even turn in your direction. You want me to explain this but as I've said, I never will. I believe you remember the dark passionflower I read about to you, the one Funes held in his hands and saw as no one ever saw it before. How beautiful it was—separate, beyond explanation. We understand so little, our minds mostly dark to us, unwilling.

If you could truly accept that passionflower for what it is, accept it as Funes once did, if you could hold it unquestioning and safe inside your mind...

Suddenly she was silent again. The miles between us black as ice.

Over the next days, if it could be said I lived in days anymore—I didn't know what to call the units of time in which I breathed—sometimes I thought I heard the beginnings of her voice, but soft, cloud-like, almost on the edge of non-existence. But then the sound would disappear. A lonely feeling crept through me.

Then once again I heard her speaking.

When I read to you, I tried to bring you facts—the world as it is and how it works. Even with Borges—there is no greater realism than his. I remember I pointed this out to you.

And now, if we consider the universe—what it is, how it functions—we must admit that everything inside it is moving away from everything else. Its nature is increasing distance, isolation. Stars pull away from other stars, planets pull away from planets. It's just how it is. I believe you have thought about this too.

So why is it so strange that I stopped speaking to you? Why should we grow close when all the universe is filled with an increasing distance? Why should you and I be the exception?

From where I stand on the edge of my black hole, I think about the many forms of distance, its varied shapes and sizes. How silence also is a form of distance. It is as natural as rocks and trees. So why can't you accept it? Think of Paul Dirac—he spoke so infrequently his colleagues said a dirac *is speech at the speed of one word per hour.*

You act as if distance and silence are unnatural, some sort of violation, but they're not.

Or consider the distance between the sun (its diameter a billion meters), and a molecule on Earth (a mere billionth of a meter)—they are worlds apart and yet that molecule still experiences the reality of the sun, could not exist without it.

The very existence of atoms depends on forces deep inside them they are ignorant of and yet those forces drive them. What's most intimate and essential is also most opaque and distant.

In any case, everything gives way to entropy in the end, it's just how it is. Think of melting ice that changes from form to formlessness. I believe you feel this in yourself, how everything inside you moves toward dissolution, the chill of non-existence. You feel it but you don't want to feel it. You don't want to believe it is true. Maybe this is why my silence bothered you. Maybe this is why you needed Funes' heartbeat close to yours. Even as you feel things break apart, you want to believe in coherence. But all over the Earth ice fields are melting, chaos blooms slowly, invisibly, then more rapidly than the eye can see. We are governed by such laws and cannot change them. Even your black hole can't release itself from isolation...Think of the lost places inside us, the many wastelands we carry.

She briefly paused, then continued.

It is very hard to know what is inside and what is outside us, and how to understand the difference. Is it even possible to know? I often thought about this as we read.

Just think of it, before 1891, the word neuron *didn't even exist. These essential parts of us unnamed. All those centuries before Wilhelm Waldeyer who was said to "have a feeling for words" came up with both* neuron *and* chromosome *as he sought to pinpoint the essential components of the brain: "Each brain cell synthesizes a specific set of molecules—proteins, lipids, polysaccharides."*

Around that same time, Camillo Golgi experimented with immersing neurons in silver nitrate until they turned black, and years before him, Joseph Von Gerlach stained them with gold chloride. Ramon y Cajal drew them from observation by the hundreds. These hidden places inside us.

I find it beautiful that they did this.

And if, as they thought, we are little more than collections of electro-chemical energy, what is loneliness? What is thought?

"Each brain is embedded in a world of other brains." I can't remember who said this. But the point is it is the very nature of neurons to be responsive to other neurons outside them. And so none of us is really alone.

Even as you believe my silence left you in a separateness you could hardly bear, it isn't really so.

You traveled through black space believing you were alone, but your neurons never believed this.

In a sense I've been with you all along.

It was so strange to hear her voice again. I kept waiting for the silence to return, but for reasons I couldn't understand, she continued.

I thought the things we read would help you see you are a creature of Earth, one infinitesimal speck in a web so intricate and vast we can never really know it.

That you are part of a system just as the stars are part of theirs. That the stars and you are part of the same system.

One afternoon I read to you about colliding stars, how they detonate violently in a dense stellar system— you have probably seen this by now—while at the same time there are other, smaller stars that meet in soft collisions. *They meld into each other, coalesce into one larger, vibrant star.*

Maybe thought is also like this. Detonating, melding, colliding.

But after I stopped speaking to you, you could see only the detonations. You could only think of leaving Earth.

So much of thinking is ignorant and blind. I do not exempt myself from this blindness.

Maybe you remember when I told you about the Fornax constellation. It appears to the naked eye as a tiny speck of black space the size of a single grain of sand—but when looked at through an infrared telescope, it contains 10,000 galaxies.

What we see is almost nothing of what is.

What if my not-speaking was like that distant constellation and you couldn't see the galaxies inside it.

Maybe you have thought about this, but maybe you haven't.

Even now I often think of how when Camillo Golgi placed dried nerve tissue under his microscope, he described the black filaments in his notebook: "some smooth, some spiny, stellate, fusiform!" The exclamation point is his. That raw sense of astonishment and wonder. "They are so delicate," he wrote, "they could easily be mistaken for ink drawings on translucent Japanese paper. They so trouble and confound the eye."

Think of those words: trouble, confound.

And think of how the neurons look. What is delicate is also strong. How else would you have survived your black hole?

No matter how many slides he looked at, Golgi knew the brain's mysteries are endless.

Maybe meaning lies in the not-understanding, in the ways things shut us out. All the ways that we remain unknowing.

A black wind swept around Sister Gudrun's body, it was wrapping her from head to foot. It seemed it should muffle her voice but it didn't.

That day I introduced you to Funes, it didn't occur to me you would take him into your fever. That you would condemn him in that way. His hurt, immobilized body. His skin airless, dull, but his mind was on fire. You even tried to keep his heartbeat close to yours.

But why tie him to your blackness like that? You who felt so hurt at being shunned, and yet you drew him toward the very things you claim have hurt you—silence, isolation.

You equipped him with a computer, nothing more. Left him alone in a bare room. Do you think that was a right thing to do?

But all of that is over now. You don't even know if he's alive.

Still, even now you like to imagine carrying him to the window. You long for his heartbeat next to yours. Once you were even tempted to tell him that like him you have no father. But consider how heavy that word father is, how heavy it would feel to him, how burdensome, far heavier than the pyramids with their weight of centuries. That word he would never be able to forget.

Words are cruelties.

Of course, I know you think silence is much worse. That my silence is the most cruel and horrible thing.

But maybe there is another way to look at it. Maybe there are other ways to think about what happened.

What if the truth is other than you believe, less terrible, less blunt?

In any case, aren't I speaking to you now? (Or maybe you think I'm an illusion).

But I meant to talk about Funes, not myself.

You told yourself you were concerned with his suffering, but maybe it was really yourself that concerned you, how alone you feel, how lost within a silence. I shouldn't have told you about the passionflower. I never should have mentioned it. But now it's too late...You will never know what it meant to him. No matter how many of its names you might learn, how many types of butterflies it carries.

Your pain is not his pain.

There are so many forms of cold. Just think of it. There are cold cases. Trails that go cold. The cold that is reserved, unmarked by error. Cold fury, insensate destruction, cold hearts. The cold of distance, indifference.

I never dreamed that I would be so cold.

Maybe your fever keeps you warm. But there is cold inside it also. It waits and is patient. There is nothing more patient than the cold.

It pained me to hear her talk about Funes. How she thought I had condemned him. A long silence followed, the distance between us even blacker and ice-still. Maybe she said all she wanted to say, there was no reason to say more. And anyway, deep in her heart she was probably still shunning me, and if we were still on Earth she wouldn't speak a single word.

Then I realized she was back.

Why did you think you could look into Funes' heart, know him? Do you think he would really want you to carry him in your arms to the window? Why do you need to picture that even now?

Even Camillo Golgi knew the brain's mysteries are endless, and yet you presume to look into Funes' heart and mind. Why do you think you can even begin to understand the lonely, paralyzed boy you first saw in the laundress's back room, the delicate filaments beneath his skull?

Why do you think he would want you to?

Maybe meaning lies precisely in the way it shuts you out.

Maybe that's the nature of the world.

Maybe Funes' distance from you is the truth of him, but it's a truth you don't want to accept.

You are sure he often looked at the fig tree, but why are you so sure? Maybe he only turned in that direction. Maybe he was seeing something else. Something you will never see.

She paused, and I waited. After a while I realized she was gone.

When her voice came back it was different, almost dreamy, softer.

All those years I read to you, I knew you needed to see me as devoid of any history, someone who had never been a child. As if I was like rocks or wind, a basic element, but with human feeling. Books grew like flowers from my hands. So many days of reading...the words binding us to each other and the world. They seemed so fragile sometimes, the words, as I read them, sometimes I almost feared for them though I didn't let on...it was a mystery how such fragility could also be so unbreakable and strong.

But I shouldn't speak of that now. I didn't mean to speak of it.

For a long time I heard nothing. A scrim of black dust settled in the air between us. Then:

That April morning when I found you on the orphanage steps, you had been left with no bottle or blanket, not even a scrap of paper with your name. At most you were a few days old, maybe even just a few hours. Babies had been left before, but none as young or small as you.

But what flustered me was you didn't cry.

Your face so small and smooth, and yet no sound came out.

I never liked babies, something about them unnerved me—I preferred to keep my distance. In the orphanage that wasn't always possible. Still, I aimed for the bare minimum. When I had to, I learned to respond to their cries, though in a mechanical, programmatic way. In my mind I catalogued the basic variations—whimpers, wails, etc.

So from the moment I found you, all I wanted was to hand you over to someone else. I barely looked into your eyes. You were so small and light in my arms and all I wanted was to be rid of you.

And still more time passed and you didn't cry.

Why was she telling me this? All that time we spent together on Earth, she never uttered a single word about my life. Part of me wanted to hear it but part of me didn't.

I kept thinking to myself, "Inside a black hole, time dies and space is like a foam of ashes." I couldn't remember where I learned it, but the thought pressed into the frightened space inside me, left no room to wonder who my parents were or why they didn't want me.

"If Tolstoy is deep inside a black hole and you are in another part of that black hole, higher up, you could read all of *War and Peace* before he finished writing the first sentence." Had Sister Gudrun taught me that? Had I seen it on Funes' white screen? I couldn't remember.

A desolate feeling spread inside me like a desert of black sand. Stark, unforgiving.

I wondered how many stars my black hole had devoured, if it was true that inside it time is destroyed and space is like a foam of ashes. Why must the center of the galaxy be made of unresponsive darkness?

If reality has nothing to do with thoughts or feelings, or with being wounded or being healed, or with loneliness or human hurt, what is it and what are its laws? Why are there black holes inside it?

And what was I to make of the fact that the combined electromagnetic radiation from every radio telescope ever built is too weak to melt one single snowflake?

I wasn't sure I wanted to know what Sister Gudrun might say next, if she even chose to say anything at all.

I didn't want to picture myself as an abandoned infant.

My eyes were stinging.

How could an infant be so silent? It seemed wrong, unnatural. A violation of nature.

After I brought you inside, as soon as you were settled in the nursery, I avoided you at every turn. My aversion more extreme than even I was used to. As if a shard of ice had lodged inside my heart.

And still I couldn't stop thinking of you. Thoughts I didn't want to have, and yet I had them. Nothing like that had ever happened to me before.

What were you that even hunger couldn't make you cry?

I began to think of you as a boy of stone among the other, fleshy children, a rock-piece in the form of a human newborn broken off and fallen from some ancient cliff.

It seemed you sensed the cruelty of the world, took it as a given. That in your silence you couldn't ask for kindness, knew it as illusion. These thoughts chilled me. I who was already cold. On the one hand the world's cruelty seemed too complicated for an infant to be sensing, though from another angle maybe not so complicated at all—stark, basic.

Some nights in my sleep I felt your tiny hand press and wrap around my finger. Then I'd look down and see a baby viper, or an earthworm, or even once a wild mushroom.

Each time I woke up sweating.

Though I told myself not to, sometimes I peered through the nursery window. Even from that distance, I could tell you were failing. Your arms brittle twigs, your eyelids puffy.

By then I had read about children who would rather die than cry for food and comfort. Something mysterious, uncompromising in them, pulling them away. Some kind of revulsion maybe. Or maybe even a kind of faithfulness—but to what? Maybe even a kind of music no one heard but them. Secretive, alluring. I didn't know.

It wasn't hard to realize if things didn't change you were going to die. And still I couldn't bring myself to walk through the nursery door. Each night I berated myself, told myself I had to. Promised to do it the next morning, then didn't. What was I that I turned from you in that way? Was I a monster? I observed my cruelty the way Golgi observed the neurons under his microscope, but where he saw beauty, I saw a monstrousness so condensed and opaque it had no meaning. Or no meaning I could find.

Then one day I simply walked through the nursery door. To this day I can't remember what I felt. I went over to your crib and picked you up and tried to feed you. I don't remember any tenderness. It was more like some machine in me was programmed to take action. Over the next days, as each morning I returned to the nursery, I realized there were hints of feelings, though I'm not sure what they were. Feelings like small storms inside me. I tried my best to push them away. But maybe I didn't have to, it didn't seem you sensed them, you were stone in my arms. Part of me admired your tenacity. So one day when after some hours you started to soften—you began to drink some of the formula, and looked into my face as you were drinking—something in me felt I had done a terrible thing—I had turned a stone boy into a human child. That I had betrayed you in some way. Maybe even betrayed something larger than us both. That it was wrong of me, and ignorant in ways I couldn't name.

I took away the unearthly beauty of your face. Interfered with a music I couldn't hear.

And later, not a day went by that I didn't think about this. I blamed myself, though sometimes I thought I had been right. I could never finally decide. As you got older, I suspected you began to sense that I was ice, the piece of stone left in your heart clearly knew this. But you never gave a hint. The law of entropy says this block of ice I am will melt, that something formless will replace me. But it is taking a long time.

Over the next days, I saw her black shape in the distance, vague, silent, unmoving. But by then I knew she would come back.

You had no name, and your namelessness tugged at me.

I'd never named any living thing, never wanted to. But there was something about the blankness that unsettled me. As if without a name you couldn't fully belong to the world, but still lingered at its edges, watchful and precarious. Curious but partly numb. (Maybe this reminds you of Funes.) In any case, even though you were feeding now, you still didn't cry, and I began to wonder, what if I named him, would that break the silence? Certainly stranger things had happened.

If I was bringing you into the world, I shouldn't waver but bring you the whole way.

But I still couldn't do it. Maybe I felt if I named you the gulf between us would be healed, our bond finally settled. That I would lose the mixed-up truth of stone and ice, of silence and sound. The outlaw truth of what it was.

A red rash started spreading on my skin. It itched and burned. It moved across my neck, then down my chest, my arms, my stomach, then even farther past my knees. A fiery rash like insects crawling. Each night I bathed myself in milk, gently patted the cracked and oozing skin, then let it dry in air. I took to wrapping my hands in gauze so I wouldn't scratch myself in sleep. My eyes teared, angry crusts formed on my eyelids, and nothing I did could make it stop. Except for my eyelids, my face remained untouched.

It was as if my refusal was writing itself on my skin. Or as if your silence was writing all over me, fierce, unforgiving. I decided I'd stay away from you, try to forget the whole thing, but the more I stayed away the more virulent the rash became. Punishing. Insistent. As if the rash was you and you came to me because I wouldn't go to you. Or as if it was the ice inside me, but red and burning. I didn't know if this was weirdly beautiful or terrible or both. After a while, I knew I had no choice but to go to you and name you.

Maybe then my skin would let me sleep.

So you see, when you think of my silence, there was another that preceded mine.

I was determined to name you, but when I leaned over your crib to pick you up, my arms froze in mid-air, I couldn't do it. A sudden fear swept through me, the idea that if I touched you my rash would spread onto your skin and hurt you. That I carried some sort of contagion even though the doctor said I didn't. Or maybe I myself was the contagion. That's how it felt. So I stood rigid by your crib and named you without touching you. Maybe now you would belong on Earth. Maybe now my rash would leave me. At least that's what I told myself.

I named you after the physicist Erwin Schrodinger, who wrote a book called "What is Life?", a book I had recently read. But as I thought about it afterwards I realized I named you after someone who lived as much or even more in the cosmos as on Earth, and in that way I failed you—didn't bring you wholly down to Earth as I planned, had still left you on the edge.

I had a book of names that said, "This interesting name, Erwin, is derived from a Celtic river name meaning fresh green water. Another version of it, a combination of the words for "army" and "friend" appears in the 1086 Domesday Book of Norfolk."

Erwin Schrodinger called himself an atheist but saw his scientific work as an approach to the godhead.

He pursued a lifelong interest in Hinduism, how it sees individual consciousness as a manifestation of a larger, unified consciousness pervading the whole universe. At least this part of it seemed to me a good thing.

Years later I learned that Schrodinger was often unwell, and would retreat to a sanitarium in Aosta. It was there he formulated his theory of the wave equation. But by then your name seemed wholly yours, I rarely thought of how I came to it.

I waited for the rash to subside, but it was still there, though less virulent, less like a fire rampaging over my skin.

That rash that told me I was bad, unworthy.

For a long time I still feared it would spread to you, patchy scales beginning on your neck or shoulders. That rash that would tell you what I lacked and who I was. But years later, when your rash finally came, it was flower-like and different. It had nothing to do with what I thought or who I was.

I hardly ever dreamed, but now my dreams grew intricate, consuming. As if the fading rash was speaking.

In one dream, Nikola Tesla stood on the far side of my room, his eyes averted. After a while he started speaking, "When I crossed the ocean on the SS Saturnia," he said, "I had no money. Alone in a new country, if I needed to dig a ditch I dug a ditch. Why would it matter how I lived? What was important were generators, motors, electricity, the mathematics of the eye, the beauty and suffering of pigeons. What mattered was will, concentration. I learned to focus on bringing these two things together: apparatus, method. That's what counted. The more I thought the more I asked myself, is it possible to photograph a thought, or for two minds to exchange thoughts directly, without speech? Over time, my inventions enabled new forms of understanding but also implied the near-endless reproduction of the human voice and likeness over the whole globe. This uncontrolled and virulent spread of the human haunted me. I had to accept there is no purity of thought or action. Feathers were beautiful to me but I was repulsed by human hair. I preferred to keep my distance. But now that I am dead I have come to realize that for someone who coveted and needed distance as I did, my life's work was about the eradication of distance. Closer, more immediate and efficient communication. Even as I lived alone in one dreary hotel room after another. I remember my solitary ecstasy when a fever gave me the idea of the alternating current. Think of all the metals on all the planets we'll never see. Of the theremin that plays its music without being touched." When I woke I was perplexed I'd had a dream with so much talking in it, and that I'd remembered all the words.

The next night in my dream he spoke again. "When I was alive," he said, "I knew I was nothing more than an automaton responding to external stimuli. I proved this over and over but no one believed me. The Earth and bodies behave electrically, I could observe this clearly. Even so, by some prank of the brain, strange things befell me. Out of nowhere, music suddenly flooded my ears. I heard the acceleration of particles, rotating magnetic fields, electric power in fierce oscillations under the ground. But my soul was too fragile, a spider's thread. When Mr. Morgan withdrew his backing and shattered my dreams, I fell ill. In my delirium I was a child in falling rain kissing my brother's ice-cold lips. He was 18 and had just died in a fall from a horse. A blue field alive with scintillating green flakes appeared behind my eyes. I started building a turbine in my mind, noted when it was out of balance, felt the weight and coolness of the metal. There was no clear place where I ended and the world began." Why was I having these dreams? What did they have to do with the small child I had named, my rash, your silence?

What these dreams meant I still don't know. Maybe they didn't mean anything, maybe like you and I they just existed. Existed like the trees and rocks and clouds. Like the personhood of rivers. I felt they had something to do with my rash but I couldn't say what. For months I continued bathing my skin in milk, examining my eyelids for the slightest sign. I trusted nothing, especially not my ability to heal, my own goodness. I was a nun but I believed in nothing. I kept this to myself. I dreamed of Tesla but never once heard your voice in a dream, or dreamed of you at all.

If I, not Sister Gudrun, was the silent one from the beginning, though I couldn't remember it, and I hadn't been able to talk to Funes either, did that make me more like Sister Gudrun than I thought? Her silence had seemed alien, sinister, and I still felt this, but now I wondered was I also wrong. I believed she sent me into isolation, but in her description I was isolate, different, from the start. A child of stone turned into a living boy. I didn't know what to think. Where Tesla's ears filled with music, mine filled with darkness. I waited for her to return.

There is a neurological disorder, asomatognosia, which is the unawareness of ownership of a part of one's own body. But what if there is a similar disorder, only it involves a part of someone else? Such as their voice. After I named you and still you made no sound, I proposed this to myself—that you had a voice but I couldn't hear it. If I could believe that, wouldn't my rash finally go away, dry up like a riverbed in sun. Maybe then I could be free.

But fairly quickly I knew it wouldn't.

Finally one night I looked up rash *in the dictionary.*

"Displaying or proceeding from a lack of careful consideration of the possible consequences of an action. Also, an eruption on the body."

"Something that spreads like wildfire or a series of unfortunate events."

"Rash decisions occur in the spur of the moment, often without possession of the facts. They are the opposite of balanced decisions, and are often made without considering the consequences, and any long-term outcomes."

Rash decisions, wildfire, unfortunate events, lack of careful consideration...I was sure those words had something to do with me and what was happening to my skin. "Lack of careful consideration." "Unfortunate event." I couldn't exactly put it all together but it seemed to touch something true, I knew this because the rash began to lessen.

And then it happened. You started making faint sounds, not cooing exactly, but something close, something like saying without words, I am here, I accept that I am here, that I am living in the world.

Often my skin felt very hot, but each time I checked if the rash was getting worse, I saw it receding.

You were learning to talk, you even played a little. My skin was smooth again, untroubled. And as I healed I realized there was something in you even from the start that didn't fit with the stone boy. From the very beginning something else was mixed in, not stone at all, but soft, almost botanical, tender. Every now and then I'd glimpsed it as I held you. Maybe it was why I feared my rash might hurt you. If you could open like that, if you could do that even while being mostly stone...So years later, when I started reading to you, I wondered if the more you knew the more you might be able to explain the botanical part, and what I'd glimpsed might finally be revealed to me. But of course that never happened. A flower doesn't explain itself. An eclipse, a plague, a shooting star doesn't explain.

Even so, I could see the reading meant something to you. Maybe I wasn't just ice anymore. I could give you something you needed. But back then those years were yet to come.

My rash was newly gone but its memory was still vivid on my skin. A vague threat. A warning.

Even though the rash no longer showed on me, and even though it hadn't hurt you like I feared, I started dreaming it was spreading on your skin. I was contagious after all. I thought I was safe but I wasn't. I was wrong to hold you. Each time I woke my heart was racing.

Then one night the dream was different.

I was alone in a forest, a golden light filtered down through the trees. The air was very soft, everything was quiet. A doe and her fawns stood a few yards away. At first they just stood still, the way deer can seem like statues, but then she was teaching them things—which berries to eat, where water was, how to cross the nearby road. Suddenly there was a loud, screeching roar. A truck barreled down the road and hit and killed them instantly. When I went over to them, I realized one survived and I held her in my arms. She was so stunned she didn't resist. Her body was lithe and well-nourished, tan with white spots. It was a peaceful body. Then I saw the face was burning. No amount of water I threw on it could stop it. The face burned and burned and when night came the face was still burning, it was a small terrible planet without sound, though the body stayed unharmed. I cradled the body and the flames didn't touch me.

After that, there was only one more dream. I dreamed my eyes were ice. I didn't dream again for many years.

It was hard to hear everything she was saying.

That night I dreamed she came to me as a block of pure, white ice. I didn't know how I could tell it was her, but I just did, and when I drew close I could see, below the glowing surface, the darker contours of her face—smudges of two eyes, a nose, a mouth. They seemed to have feeling.

The ice was very quiet. I waited for a long time but it didn't melt though a bright sun was shining.

After a few years, when the purple heliotropes appeared on your eyelids, I was un-nerved. I understood you found it beautiful, the rash, as if you had become *those flowers, or the flowers had chosen you to be their human host—that they trusted you in this way, knew you wouldn't hurt them. But of course it reminded me of the rash I tried so hard to forget.*

I had turned a stone boy into a boy of human flesh, but maybe I hadn't.

I realized in some vague way the heliotrope rash felt like a kind of rebuke, though I didn't know why. Then one day it came to me—it was showing me if the host were good the rash could be beautiful, not terrible like mine. If the heart were good. If the heart could open. If the heart had not recoiled from the abandoned, silent child.

I'd heard of prodigies but never met one. John Stuart Mill learned Greek and arithmetic at age three. At eight years old he knew six dialogues of Plato. At seven, the mathematician Norbert Wiener devoured books on biology and physics, and by eight his eyestrain from constant reading was so extreme the doctor forbid him to read for 6 months. He learned then entirely through listening, solving complex mathematical problems in his head. Though you were nowhere as extreme, early on I noticed you learned more quickly than I'd ever seen, sometimes it was as if the facts were air you breathed in. Shortly after your rash appeared and you were forced to spend long hours inside (your eyelids violet, your white hair) I read to you even more often. At that time your eyes were weak from your condition, you couldn't read much on your own. At first I didn't think much about it, it was just something that needed to be done. Though every now and then, when I was least expecting it, you seemed to be thinking so intently, I started to fear my rash was coming back.

It was lulling to remember the hours of our reading, all the words she brought me, I almost forgot her long silence and that I was on a black hole and black dust blew between us.

So when she disappeared, at first I didn't realize it happened. I was just waiting as I waited many times, believing she'd come back.

Long ago she told me information is never lost but only *appears to be lost*. We were reading as usual, sitting side by side by the tall window. She said this is called *coarse graining*. I didn't understand what she meant but nodded like I did. So now that she seemed to have disappeared without explanation, I wondered if what I needed to know—where she was, why she left me—existed somewhere but I couldn't reach it.

The way someplace, though my mind couldn't find it, the burning fawn was still burning.

But then it occurred to me, what if she hadn't chosen to leave, what if something happened and she couldn't come back?

What if she was hurt or dead?

A chill went through me. It didn't make sense she would choose to leave me now. It seemed she had much more to tell me.

As I stood on the Event Horizon, a chain of lonely thoughts moved through me—the woman's brainwaves travelling through interstellar space, Schwarzschild lying in his trench, suffering and dreaming. How Funes said he was a star gone wrong.

I tried to calm myself, spoke to myself inside my mind: whatever happened between us is what happens naturally to living beings: loss, misunderstanding. There was no reason to think she was dead or in some way hurt. Why should I know where she is or what has happened?

I tried to accept the blackness around me.

The lonely fear kept beating.

One meaning of silence is interference with the expression of a gene, the successful suppression of its biological function. I remembered when she read that to me.

Long ago her silence entered and changed me.

In the deepest, most secret recesses of my body, I felt it moving.

I kept wondering if she died. She had told me about the stone infant, her rash, why would she stop speaking now?

Ragged wings of drifitng ash blew past me.

When her voice came back, for a second I thought it must be a memory or hallucination.

I was relieved but at first what she was saying confused me.

I am in Antarctica. So you see now why it took so long to hear from me again. I am very far from you, it takes time for sound to travel. You will be surprised that I left my black hole, but unlike you I never meant to stay away from Earth. Did you really think I'd stay on that black hole forever? I never forgot the Earth is home.

Here in Antarctica there are no permanent residents, no towns or cities. Not one single address. So you see, it is a good place to be alone. In some ways it's like a black hole but much less extreme. The sun stays always low on the horizon, even in mid-summer. The ground is a sheet of white ice.

When all the land-ice here melts, and it will melt soon, sea level will rise 200 feet over the whole globe. So you see, like you I am standing on a site of danger and precarity. Though you may ask yourself, is there any other kind of place left on the Earth? Where on Earth is it safe to stand now?

All those years I read to you, I wanted you to wonder about such things. I taught you to question.

The ice below my feet is a faint, surprising blue. It is said this is caused by a red light inside it. I find it beautiful, this blueness.

(Maybe my rash never left me after all. Maybe it is like the red light inside the ice.)

Maybe you still wonder why I came to this cold place (you love to see me as a puzzle) where even to walk a short distance is exhausting. Or maybe by now you understand there are always many questions and few answers. And the few answers shatter.

But where else could I have brought my silence and refusal? The fact of what once passed between us.

I am very tired now. I have traveled a long way. I need to sleep.

Like the scientists who learned you must hold on to the idea that there is little or nothing to hold onto, in the hushed blackness of my mind I waited.

Did you know that no one has ever crossed Antarctica alone?

The Thiel Mountains rise like dorsal fins from a white sea. The Ronne Ice Shelf is 60 feet thick. Even in summer, temperatures plunge to 50 below. To cross the entire 921 miles would take at least sixty days of walking over ice in blasting wind.

Still, some have tried. One man prepared by spending every day for three months dragging giant truck tires along a rough riverbank. Another plunged both hands into ice-water, then forced himself to tie and untie knots. He did this for several hours each day for four weeks. But neither of them made it across.

Not long ago a man covered over 900 miles before succumbing to an infection of the leg. He was just a few days away from completion. His body was airlifted out. Infected wounds fester easily in cold, the body heals more slowly.

I stand alone here, blue sky filling my eyes. I lift one heavy foot, then the other, then pause for a few minutes. I know I am no different from the others, there is no way to cross alone.

Or maybe I'm lying when I say I am in Antarctica.

Maybe I am somewhere else.

There are many cold places in the mind.

But I'm not reaching across this distance to talk about Antarctica. It's hard work to send a voice so far.

You must wonder why I stopped speaking about your life, those early years we spent together. I am still trying to explain.

After I found myself telling you about my rash, your first days etc.—things I never dreamed I'd say—never wanted to say, had vowed I wouldn't, a strange feeling came into me like something rigid, cold, but also moving, almost like an ice shelf but cracked and breaking. At first I paid no attention, dismissed it as a passing thing.

But it wouldn't let me go. It was telling me there were even more things I had to tell you. Things I never dreamed I'd say.

I still wonder if I'm doing the right thing. It is not a simple thing to tell. At first it will just puzzle you, you will need to be patient.

But where should I begin? You will wonder what it has to do with you. But listen carefully and eventually you will come to understand.

There is an experimental laboratory in Geneva, near CERN, not far from the orphanage where we lived.

You might be surprised how many such laboratories exist over the globe. Many of them are kept completely secret. Some specialize in the manipulation of viruses. Others concentrate on cloning. Still others on artificial organs, the mapping and manipulating of the brain.

They are asking fundamental questions: Can human intelligence be moved outside the human body? What interfaces might exist between the human mind and machines? In what ways might human minds and machines eventually blend into each other? And just how private is the human mind? Does it need to be private? What is consciousness anyway and where does it reside? Can thoughts be read by observing neurons? What changes can be made to DNA?

Many of these labs are like Antarctica that seems little more than a blank whiteness, devoid of any specific addresses. They exist in hiddenness only, not meant to be found out. And the majority of experiments eschew human subjects, are carried out on small organisms like snails or bacteria, or even on larger mammals like monkeys and cats, or by computer modeling.

But in rare cases there are human subjects. Technically this is not allowed, but it happens.

You will recall the Geneva Convention laid out the rights of the experimental subject, remember when I read it to you? But conventions aren't facts, laws and protections aren't facts.

This is what I am trying to tell you (though even now a good part of me pulls back.) A few years after I took charge at the orphanage, I was approached by a prominent businessman. He explained the need for experimental subjects in the name of progress and for the good of all humankind. Orphaned children were the best. No one looks for them or keeps track of them. He promised none would come to harm. Not once, not ever. Not even in the smallest way. The orphanage was full of children no one missed or remembered. He asked me to agree to help him.

At first I told him no, but he came back several times. He offered funds to keep the orphanage afloat in perpetuity, for school and job training, even to build a new building in another city.

Over the next years I sent him a few children. Some years I sent just one, some years none at all. I never heard what became of them. Just once a child came back, quiet, with a bandaged eye. His right hand moved slowly. But even then I said nothing.

Of course I should have known better. I knew about the Milgram experiment that tested obedience to authority by having willing participants agree to inflict what they believed were painful shocks on another participant behind a partition. Even when they felt it was wrong to do it and could hear the seeming cries of the one they thought they were hurting and didn't want to go on, they continued. I was like them, but worse. Willfully ignorant, self-blinding.

One day two scientists visited from the laboratory. A man and a woman. They could see you learned more quickly than the others. Maybe your illness also interested them, I didn't know. I let you think they wanted to adopt you. For several months they visited, brought you books and toys, and as you played they made their observations. At that point I still wasn't sure what they were after. Then one day they explained they needed to take you with them. I stood there and said nothing. They asked me to pack your things and I did. You were the only person in the world I felt close to, and yet I did this to you. I didn't say a single word.

When I came back with your suitcase, the man and woman went off to a corner and talked. The man talked several times on his cell phone. And then without explanation, they changed their minds. They left without you and never came again.

But I had seen who I was, what I was capable of doing, what I'd done. How could I keep reading to you, how could I look in your direction? The silence spread like the red rash from long ago inside me, every day it grew more virulent, more fiery and terrible. No matter how hard I tried I couldn't stop it. Even as I shunned you and you stayed inside your room. Even as I watched you sicken.

How could I take in what she was saying? I needed her to stop, to let me be alone with what she'd said, though mostly I wished I never heard it, but instead of pausing she kept talking.

I was hot and dizzy but forced myself to listen.

Maybe now you see why I came to this cold place where there is no one I can hurt or betray, though every now and then I glimpse the distant evidence of human life—the steel ladders of the Ice Cube Neutrino Observatory. Neutrinos rarely interact with matter, but as they travel through this ice faster than the speed of light, they leave behind shockwaves like waves on water, and the Observatory detects them. In one year alone, twenty-eight originating outside the Solar System have been detected.

So you see, in a way I am like you—I live among particles now. These beings that don't know or care if I exist. (Though I know you believed your antiparticles were deeply feeling beings.)

But I was telling you about the day I agreed to send you away. The day everything changed.

Soon after my terrible act of betrayal, like a judgment on me the rash came back. That rash I had dreaded for so long. At first I tried to convince myself it was only my fear not my skin I was feeling. But maybe they are the same thing.

It was like watching my mind writing on my skin. My mind made visible. A poisoned wing of thought touching down in one place then another. Tireless, driven.

After a while I told myself it was justice I was seeing, and it was.

The rash spread over my neck and moved into my eyes. It stung them and I couldn't see. You were deep in your fever by then. Borges described his blindness as a gray mist with yellow tinges, but mine was a deep black, sometimes there were flecks of red. I lived in it for weeks, that blackness. Only a few times when I was dreaming, in my mind I could still see. But even then in my dream I closed my eyes.

One morning I woke and I could see again. It was that sudden. The rash had vanished. Everything as clear as before.

I went on with my life as if nothing happened.

Before I came here, a man claimed to have finally crossed Antarctica without a companion or outside assistance. But others dispute this. Years before, his legs and feet were burned in a terrible accident, he'd gotten tangled in a burning rope and was told he would never walk without crutches. But he refused to accept this. For years he trained, growing stronger, pulling sleds piled with heavy sand along various beaches, and when it was time for his crossing, for two months he pulled his sled over the ice with provisions weighing 300 lbs. No one disputes this, just the idea that he did it without help as his route included a stretch of man-made path.

Though his legs healed long ago, he says the fire is still inside them, he can feel it burning. Every second he still feels it.

My rash is like that. It vanished but it also didn't. I know what I did to the children, to you. The ones I sent away, and you whose suitcase I readied for the journey. Even though they didn't take you.

What right did I have to look you in the eye, to speak to you, after that? The shard of ice in my heart was larger than I thought. Harder, stronger.

What right do I have to speak even now?

And still I think of those hours of our reading. Our chairs, the tall window.

I could see her again, or what seemed to be her, a small figure buried to the shoulders in black snow, the wild black air around her swirling. It didn't look like the Antarctica she described. I didn't know where she was.

So what was truth and what was lies? I knew I'd never know.

Part of me wanted to comfort her, but my heart felt heavy, my wrists encircled with a weight like shackles. My tongue lifeless, numb.

I was waiting but didn't know for what.

Finally when she spoke again it seemed many hours had passed.

I am leaving you, she said. *There is nothing left for me to tell you. Whatever you make of all this, you will come to it on your own, without me.*

You'll never know what I think or where I am. All of that is over now. It's just how it is.

I never knew why you trusted me. Why you listened so deeply and so well. Even that first day when I found you on the steps with no name or belongings, I looked into your eyes and for a moment you looked back at me with trust. Even though you made no sound. I see that now, though for so long I didn't want to see it. I told you I didn't look into your face then but I did. It was as if you saw a mild place inside me, something almost warm and willing. And later when I read to you, sometimes I almost thought it could be true. But mostly I had no illusions.

We understand so little.

I remember how you waited for the antiparticles to come for you and take you away. You thought I didn't know this but I did. And how you heard the footprints on the moon softly crying. You used to say these things in your sleep. I stood outside your door and listened.

Once you thought you saw me, but when you looked again there was only a black cage.

So how could you ever trust what you were seeing?

How do you know if I am even speaking to you now? Or if what I say is truthful?

Each brain is embedded in a world of other brains. I remember when I read that. So it seems impossible there can be so much aloneness, yet there is.

I think of Golgi's dyed neurons like delicate ink drawings on translucent Japanese paper. Of recorded brainwaves travelling alone through outer space. And of all those books we read, the two of us in our chairs by the window.

Often I still think of Funes' passionflower, though I don't know why I think of it. Maybe because it meant so much to you. And of the fig tree in the garden. His ruined legs. His lovely mind on fire. The barred window.

You still believe my silence drove you from the world, maybe you will never stop believing it. Maybe it is even true. But where does that get you?

The air is growing even colder now. I never knew that I could be so cold. I still see the passionflower.

The silence was different now. Smoother, colorless, detached. I understood that she was gone forever.

II. THE CYBORG

The whole sky was a white screen, and inside it Funes' heart was beating. Though I couldn't see it, I knew it was there.

Its sound was the thinnest edge between something and nothing, the barest cusp of nonexistence.

I opened my eyes. The white sky was still there but the heartbeat had vanished. I didn't know where I was.

My head ached, I wasn't sure if I was looking at a ceiling or the sky.

I realized I was back on Earth.

Behind my eyes, I still saw the orphan planets drifting in their cauls of ice.

Many days passed, I wasn't sure how many. Once I thought I heard a bird, but when I looked there was nothing.

Was anyone even alive on the Earth?

The longer I lay there, the more fearful I became.

It is the business of the future to be dangerous, I remembered those words from Funes' screen. There was so much I didn't know, almost everything.

Everywhere I looked, the ground was bare and flat, the air completely still.

I had fallen a long way. I was unsure if I could stand or walk. Maybe I was paralyzed like Funes.

Ludwig Boltzmann said nothing is more difficult than emptiness. It seemed I had landed in an emptiness that was boundless and would last forever.

It was then the Cyborg came to me.

His eyes were cloudy gray and very kind. Even the whites were pale gray. A crimson scar like a bolt of frozen lightening ran down his waxen cheek. A blood spot dotted his right eye.

His scalp looked like a patchwork of tectonic plates, as if a clumsy hand had taken it apart and carelessly shoved it back together. Behind his left ear was a black, rectangular box the size of a memory stick but half as thick.

His right hand looked stiff and misshapen.

I hadn't sensed him walking toward me. When I looked up, he was just there.

After a few seconds, he looked into my eyes, and started speaking.

I watched you in the courtyard, he said. *At first I thought I would just watch for a few minutes, but then the minutes turned into hours and the hours into days, the days turned into weeks. I never meant for it to happen, it just did. I stood beneath the oak tree, thinking you would see me, but you never did. Sometimes you even looked in my direction.*

I had been walking for several days when I glimpsed the cistern in the courtyard. I meant only to stop for water then move on. It was late afternoon, the sun was dimming. At first the courtyard looked empty, I thought everyone had gone inside. But then I saw you on a bench, an open book in your hands. I waited for you to go in.

I was used to waiting. I had done it all my life.

Before that time, I'd never once seen sunlight. All I knew was laboratory glass, microsensors, fMRI scans, EEG's, all sorts of metals and component parts. Walls lined with video monitors, drawers filled with silver instruments and latex gloves. A narrow room with one small bed and a surveillance camera. There was one other, larger room, completely white—I spent many hours there each day. In the lab there were no mirrors—I saw many scans and x-rays of my brain, but never my own face. I was there as an experimental subject. Like you, I lived behind a wall.

I will not tell you now how or why I left there, only that as I stood beneath the oak tree watching, a strange feeling came into me— I didn't want to leave you. Why couldn't I make myself leave? The feeling was unfathomable even to me. All I knew was you were suffering, I could feel it. I didn't know how I knew it, but I did. Your skin was pale, there were dark crescents underneath your eyes, but mostly nothing showed.

That night, I found an unlocked toolshed where I slept.

The next morning, I returned to my place beneath the oak tree. Several weeks passed in this way. My days were spent watching you, my nights lying on the toolshed floor, thinking and dreaming.

Often I felt serene as I watched. As if being near you was something I was meant to do, though I didn't know why or even really what it was. To all appearances it looked like I was doing nothing. Each day I felt closer to you, though I reminded myself I didn't know you.

And then one afternoon as I stood beneath the oak tree, a sudden feeling came into me—I understood you were falling ill and you didn't know it. Like before, I didn't know how I knew this, I just did. Your sickness had cold stars in it, black flowers. It was the loneliness of antiparticles and discarded machines, the detritus of some monstrous logic. And all the while you kept sitting on the bench and reading. The jar of pebbles by your side grew fuller, sometimes you picked up a pinecone, turned it over a few times, then put it down. Every now and then you looked into the distance. I never saw you speak. For awhile I tried to tell myself I was mistaken, that what seemed like sickness was really something else—or that maybe I'd just made it all up. But each time I tried to tell myself these things, a thin blade of warning glittered in my chest.

The sickness moved in slow, gentle waves through your body. Secretive, clandestine. And still I knew there was a blade in it and that blade would hurt you. Even as you looked away. Even as you didn't feel it.

For a second, I lowered my eyes. When I looked up again, he was gone.

I turned my head to one side then the other, but no matter where I looked there was only miles of empty sky and flat, brown land. No trace of him anywhere. Why had he come if he didn't mean to stay beside me? Given all he said, it made no sense he would just leave. I was sure I saw him clearly.

In the darkness of my mind, I pictured his kind eyes.

Several days passed. I still waited for him, though more and more I believed he wasn't coming back.

If I stayed very still, maybe then he would see his appearance didn't scare me, I hadn't tried to run away. Maybe then he would come back. But I'd already been very still, barely turned my head. I didn't know what other signal I could send.

As I waited I wondered, how could he even live in the world? Who would bother to try to understand him? At the first sight of his red scar, black box and waxen skin, wouldn't they recoil, or even run? As if his strangeness was a kind of crime.

But why did he even look the way he did?

I wondered if he was the result of an experiment gone wrong. A botched attempt at something else, something better. That would be one explanation. That he was a misstep, a failure. Maybe the lab had discarded him. And maybe that's why he'd been walking without food or water. Maybe that's why he was alone.

And yet so much of him seemed right—he looked strong, his eyes were kind, he hadn't wanted to scare me.

I tried to imagine how it felt to live inside his body. Were there microchips implanted in his brain? Synthetic cells mixed in with human tissue? How much of him was engineered, how much inborn, and could he feel the difference? Did he carry a loneliness like mine? Had someone named him?

I wondered about the committees, grant proposals, data sets that must have led up to what he had become. How it seemed the softest and most quiet violence, that living beings would tamper with another living being and alter and regulate his parts.

But I didn't know if any of my thoughts were even close to what was true. It had grown late. The sky was darkening.

In my mind's eye I saw his clouded eyes.

More days passed. The land looked even emptier, the sky more vast. Then suddenly he was back.

I tried not to think of you, he said, *I tried very hard to stay away. But I keep talking to you in my mind.*

Last time after I left you, I told myself I had been wrong to come to you. Wrong to let you see my cloudy eyes and long, red scar, the black box behind my ear, this skull like a broken bowl stuck back together. This botched, metallic hand. What good could it do you? And I had left you so abruptly. You must have wondered why I came at all.

But I kept remembering those days in the courtyard, when I realized you were failing and I just stood beneath the oak tree and did nothing. I didn't even try to help you. So what did it matter what I noticed or what I felt? I never tried to warn you or bring comfort. Each day you grew more distant and alone. I was afraid if you saw me you would run away. But I was cowardly not to even try. I told myself I should be different now, not turn away.

And still I wondered, Why did no one realize you were sickening?

Sister Gudrun walked with slow, measured steps in the courtyard and acted like she didn't see you. Once I saw her turn in your direction, then abruptly turn away.

It was clear her silence pained you.

As I said, back then I stood there and did nothing.

And then one afternoon, your fever came just like I knew it would—your eyelids swelled, your bones turned soft as water.

I wanted to tell him I was glad he was back, that his face didn't scare me, but when I tried to speak my mouth was dry, no sound came from my throat.

I tried to show him with my eyes.

Then I tried to speak again, and again no words came out. I had no explanation.

It was like watching Funes—how I could never speak a single word to him or let him know I cared that he existed. And in that silence he grew weaker and then disappeared.

I wanted to tell the Cyborg it didn't matter if he was born or constructed or a combination, either way I could still sense his goodness.

I wished I could tell him what I thought.

The Cyborg continued:

Back then I passed many nights in the toolshed planning how when the time was right I'd finally come to you in your fever and you wouldn't be afraid. You would lie there in your burning skin and believe I was unreal, a figment, a delusion, nothing that could ever hurt you. You'd believe your fever invented me, I could dissolve at any moment, and in that way you wouldn't need to be afraid. It would be safe to stand just inches from you, and speak of the courtyard, the cistern, how I watched you. And of how something inside me felt you sicken. I would speak to you of loneliness and stars and planets, and maybe of many beautiful things I hadn't yet thought of. And those things would calm you. You'd understand you weren't alone. That someone cared and was beside you.

But after your fever came, once it was actually happening, a new shame spread through me. I knew almost nothing of the world, had never even spoken to anyone out loud. So how could I think I had anything to give you?

What did I know beyond the lab? Why did I believe anything I'd say could help you?

I convinced myself that in its way the fever was protecting you. Wasn't it what you wanted all along even if you didn't know it? I had no right to interfere. I wasn't even wholly human. I didn't know what I was.

I watched you from a distance, silent, not moving.

But even as I stayed away I wasn't sure I was doing the right thing. Your fever showed no sign of stopping, you had grown even thinner, I finally told myself I wasn't convinced the fever was protecting you, it seemed wrong to leave you alone. Wasn't that why I'd stayed under the oak tree in the first place—there was some bond between us. I didn't know you, yet deeply felt you in ways I couldn't explain. It seemed time to be beside you.

Every day I thought of how there are distances inside you I would never know, and those distances made you beautiful to me. You were nothing I could summarize or own. You were embodied, difficult, messy, mysterious, not free. I couldn't make you into something that would fit into a way of seeing. Many nights I imagined drawing toward you, watching the slightest shiver of an eyelid, wondering how you felt, if you were dreaming. Sister Gudrun's silence, had it dissolved inside you? Were you relieved to be away from the courtyard? Or in your mind were you still there? "The nature of the universe is distance and isolation." I had read this. But increasingly that seemed not quite right. Isn't it also tenderness, longing, proximity, collision?

In any case I finally came.

I reminded myself you had no idea I had been watching. So the intimacy I felt would be alien to you. Maybe the sight of me would scare you. But I knew I had to try.

As I said, I'd never spoken to anyone. At least not in the only life I remember—my life inside the lab. Who I was before or how I ended up there—all of that was lost to me long ago. Whatever was done to me there took all of that away, though in the end their algorithms failed, their methods were lacking. I didn't turn out as they wanted.

Even before I saw you, I had many feelings I didn't understand—had no remembered history to attach them to, and yet my feelings hadn't left me. It was strange to feel I was myself but have no memory of who that was.

A hurt wing moved in my chest. Something in me grieved and listened.

How can I begin to tell you? I barely know how to tell it to myself. And why am I telling you? Do I believe my tale will somehow calm you? But what else can I speak of to you, what else do I know? I want to give you the sense that we are here together.

Like me, I think you understand that feeling of being oneself and not, present and not. Like me, your origins are dark. You don't know your parents, who they were, if they named you. Why they let you go.

I guess I could try to start at the beginning (though even now, I'm not sure where that is.)

How can I explain what living in the lab was like? The mixture of ignorance and knowledge it entailed. How I lived in darkness mixed with light.

The lab took pride in what it called its "humane, participatory ethos." So even though I was an experimental subject without rights, they wanted me to know about the human brain. The very parts of me they'd altered. As if we were collaborators, as if I had some role in my own unwilling transformation.

But all that really meant was learning what they taught me and doing what they wanted me to do.

I didn't understand what good could come of it, it seemed learning about brain anatomy and function could only make me grieve—but I learned what they taught me. How the brain is a collection of electrochemical signals activating a network of cells for the extraction of patterns to which it assigns meanings and interpretations. Right now as I'm standing beside you, your brain has decided the pattern of abstract shapes you are seeing equals me. It has assigned to it that meaning. And my brain has done the same to you.

But even as I learned what they taught me, it felt partly hollow, incomplete. It was like seeing a black and white video. I was sure something was missing.

But I've been talking much too long. I didn't mean to tire you. I'm still not used to my own voice. Your fever is still high, you need to sleep.

In my dream Funes' computer screen was floating in the air above me. It was blank and terrible, and my heart ached as I watched it. Then I saw him on his narrow cot. I was so happy to see him. But as I stepped closer, I realized he was the Cyborg and where his heart should have been, a small red bird turned in slow circles dragging its red, broken wing. A few times it tried to fly but couldn't. How could he live with a wounded bird for a heart?

When I woke, I wondered where he was and when he would come back.

Afte a while I realized his comings and goings didn't mean he'd leave me. (I thought of Sister Gudrun on her back hole, how she came back many times.) Though where he spent his nights I never knew, and always I felt relieved when I heard him.

He talked more about the courtyard.

But I'm not ready to talk about the lab. At least not that directly. Those weeks I watched you in the courtyard, I could see what you were reading. My eyes, though cloudy, possess a strong acuity, much more powerful than a natural human eye. In the lab I'd spent many hours at the computer looking up many things, but the world outside was still new to me, there was so much I didn't know. So as you read, I read with you.

One afternoon you started a new book. It was Maeterlinck's The Life of the Bee.

As soon as I read the first page, I began to feel dizzy. "The successful beekeeper peacefully violates the secret chambers. Without the bees' knowledge, he furtively restricts or augments their births and regulates fecundity. Without their becoming discouraged or impoverished, he deprives them of the fruits of their labor. In a word, he does with them what he will, and obtains what he will, provided what he seeks is in accordance with their laws and virtues."

The words kept revolving in my mind: "Peacefully violates." "Furtively." "Deprives." (But how can violation be peaceful?)

Was the whole world a lab? And every being an experimental subject like myself? I had left the lab, but it seemed that I was still inside it.

I wondered what you felt as you read. You closed the book. As you headed back inside, your left leg was dragging.

That night back in the toolshed, I slept a restless, troubled sleep, my head buzzing with the sound of bees. So the next afternoon when you opened Maeterlinck's book, I told myself to turn away.

And still I read what you were reading.

But this time it was different. It was about the bees themselves:

"When it's time, the bees abandon the hive they have so painstakingly built, leaving it for a future generation. This is the true spirit of the beehive: they live in obedience to a law higher than their own happiness. Having attained the utmost pinnacle of prosperity and power, they willingly fly off into the hardships and perils of a new and distant country. They leave behind the fruits of their labor, their wealth and their home, for the generation to come. No matter the strength of the kingdom she makes, the Queen's life ends in exile and poverty."

This seemed very beautiful to me. It was like glimpsing the goodness of the world. For a split-second, the lab's antiseptic light crumbled inside me.

The next afternoon when I returned, the book was on the bench beside you. I read its back cover: BY THE SAME AUTHOR ALSO AVAILABLE IN HOLIDAY EDITIONS: THE TREASURE OF THE HUMAN, THE WRATH OF THE STORM, WISDOM AND DESTINY, THE DOUBLE GARDEN.

You picked it up, turned to a highlighted passage: "We watch the bees hasten from flower to flower and imagine we know them. But even if we draw near, the eye meets only the enigma of destiny and will, the incomprehensible nature of the smallest-seeming actions."

I felt like small scars were opening all over my body. I was a secret from myself. And the secret had a hurt in it, a darkness.

But maybe I shouldn't talk about those days when I watched you. You are still weak with fever. And anyway, it seems wrong to talk about myself, but as I said before, when I think of what to say to you, it's the one story I know well enough to tell. I could leave you to your dreams, your silence. But every time I tell myself that's best, I remember how in the courtyard you seemed so alone. It feels wrong to leave you.

Maybe it doesn't matter what I say as long as you can hear my voice and know I'm beside you.

Still, it is hard to know what to say next. If I say more about the lab, I am taking you down a path you may not want to go. I don't want to hurt you.

I hope what I'm saying is better than leaving you alone.

(Sometimes at night I almost feel myself dissolving. I wonder if you feel this too.)

As I said before, the lab's ethos was for me to feel included. But very soon it wasn't hard to see, as is so often the case, its need to proclaim its "humane, participatory ethos" arose from the fact the very opposite was happening.

So although I learned what they taught me, mostly I felt left in my own darkness. I kept wondering, What exactly did they do to me and why? Why am I constructed as I am? What do they have planned for me? What are they hoping to accomplish? All these things they never spoke of. (They never wanted me to speak.) A few times when they sensed my growing wariness (monitors on my scalp kept track), they assured me my questions would eventually be answered, that all they could presently say was I was part of something called the Empathy Project and I should take comfort in the fact my life had meaning, I was serving the good of humankind, of science.

I wanted to believe this, but something in me didn't.

And since I never spoke—they didn't want me to speak—I kept this to myself.

The lab was named NeuroSpin, its mission "the advancement and acceleration of the understanding of the human brain." This involved two main components: the comprehension and treatment of brain disorders, and the development of new hybrid and brain-like technologies. Its co-founders were Jose Delgado, Denis Le Bihan and Stanislas Dehaene, but by the time I was there they were long gone. All I knew was their departure was abrupt and they'd left willingly, all at the same time. They must have packed in a great hurry—an entire bookcase filled with Dehaene's books was left behind, there were papers on his desk.

Dr. Le Bihan was renowned for his invention of the diffusion MRI which measures the molecular motion of water through biological tissues. He described his work as " the study of the nature of the brain from mouse to man."

Dr. Dehaene was an expert in the neural correlates of consciousness. (It took me a while to discover what that is.)

Dr. Delgado manipulated the brain's electrical impulses of pleasure and pain to influence behaviour. "The successful remote control of activities in several species through brain manipulation has now lead us toward the ultimate objective of developing such systems for human application." (This sounded very troubling, but at least at first I just tried to take it in.)

From the start, their combined strengths made NeuroSpin an important center for brain research.

But with the founders gone, I wasn't sure what it was after. I moved among its surveillance cameras, its walls of video monitors and humming machines with no idea of who I was or why I was there. Sometimes I touched the long scar on my face, the narrow box on my scalp. But nothing I touched or saw could tell me who I was or why I was there.

Without any firm grounding (except for the vague name of the Empathy Project) very soon I began to believe there was something wrong with me.

I was human and not, a commodity and not, a secret, an outcome, a dark dream. My eyes were cloudy, my hand irregular.

At first it came as a vague suspicion. My invasive questioning thoughts seemed to me a kind of sign my brain had turned out wrong. That I was a failed experimental subject in some way. And as I said, I noticed my right hand was slightly malformed and larger than my left, and its skin had a faint metallic cast. Why would they give me a hand like that? All I could think was I hadn't turned out right.

Maybe it's the nature of the real to evade a firm foothold. There's suspicion but not fact. Wariness, fear, intuition.

Nights I lay awake, ashamed of what I was. Each secret thought a kind of crime.

Mornings, I checked my right hand. Maybe overnight it had become a normal hand. Even as I checked, I knew this was foolish.

Sometimes I dreamed of black holes. They followed me into my waking silence. Their fierce emptiness shining.

What is an "I"? Is it even one thing or several? The longer I wondered, the more weird and unfathomable identity became. Cut loose from my history, how could I know who I was?

It felt like the world was dissolving around me—delicate, too porous, partly vanished. Though something in me still longed to hold it.

Where did this tenderness come from? This longing for a world I had no access to and didn't know?

One day in the hallway I overheard parts of a conversation. Something about "cognitive waywardness," "neural imprecision", "too sensitive, too many questions" followed by terms I didn't recognize that had to do with human-machine interaction, transhuman beings, artificially intelligent weapons.

Right away I was convinced they were talking about me. I understood "too sensitive, too many questions" but the mention of weapons left me baffled. What did weapons have to do with me?

Right then I made my decision—I couldn't wait for explanations. I needed to find some things out.

Late that night, after the custodians finished cleaning, I walked down the darkened hallway and, using my small flashlight as a guide, slipped quietly into Dehaene's old office. I wasn't sure what I was looking for. Some hint, maybe, of the thoughts behind the experiment that made me. I had nothing specific in mind. I just needed a beginning.

There was a handwritten notecard on Dehaene's old desk. "Consciousness is nothing more than the circulation of information within a switchboard of critical neurons."

Could that be all I, or anyone, is and would ever be—information within a switchboard? But if that was so, where did my loneliness come from? Why did I have any feelings at all?

My feeling of being botched—did that come from information I knew but didn't know I knew? I supposed it could.

A metal bookcase spanned an entire wall. It held monographs, books, bound collections of articles and reports. On one shelf alone there were three years worth of professional journals: PLoS Biology, NeuroImage, Cognition, Developmental Science.

Off to itself, on a small round table, was Changeux's L'Homme neurona (Neuronal Man: The Biology of the Mind) *which Dehaene credited as his greatest influence and inspiration.*

Pink sodium light filtered in from the parking lot outside. The hour passed quickly. I knew I would have to return another time.

Over the next several nights I returned to Dehaene's old office.

I read about computational neuronal models of human cognition. Of functional neuroimaging and a global neuronal workspace. About lesions in the parietal lobe that lead to impaired multiplication but preserve subtraction. About visual word form areas, ventral stream regions, the connection between numbers and space.

And all the while I wondered, would any of it lead to some knowledge of myself.

Mostly I didn't understand what I was reading, but something of the feeling came through. It was a feeling of wonder mixed with an unease, a darkness.

One night, flipping randomly through one of Dehaene's old books, I came across a note on lined paper:

"We are trying to understand the physical mechanisms that allow us to have an inner world. Brain imaging is finally exposing this inner territory which has existed far too long in near-total obscurity."

But weren't there parts of me, of anyone, that didn't want to be known? Didn't want to be dragged up into a world of use, exposure, relentless visibility?

When does knowing become a violation?

Part of me felt the desire to know and understand is logical, even beautiful. But part of me wondered.

I thought of the desire to explore—rockets to the moon, the northern explorers—those seemed a good thing. Facts transcend desire. Facts seem the one thing you can trust—impervious, given. So shouldn't it be good to know them? The structure and workings of the brain are facts—changes in blood flow, the medial prefrontal cortex, etc. And still something nagged at me, a feeling of trespass, violation.

The scientists at the lab knew more about my history than I knew myself. They knew how I came to be as I am—who I was, what steps were taken. And they kept getting more information from the sensors attached to my head, the black box, the many tests they gave me.

The Helsinki Declaration insists "the well-being of the individual research subject must take precedence over all other interests." Research must "promote respect for all human subjects," and "protect the subjects' dignity, integrity, privacy and right to self-determination." In article 22, it states all participation must be voluntary. But I knew from my own life that isn't true.

What would the world be like with inner lives laid bare and subject to being altered? Isn't it the nature of the human face to reveal but also conceal. (At that time, I'd never even seen my own face.)

That night before I returned to my room, I found another piece of paper. "The Stentrode brain computer interface project has now proved that through use of the brain alone a human subject can control a Surface Book2, sending text messages and emails. However, some of the subjects report behavioral side effects which require looking into—compulsive gambling, apathy, hallucinations."

When I got back to my room, my mind was reeling.

He had stopped speaking. As I pictured him rummaging in Dehaene's old office, finding scraps that left him troubled, and lying in his bed convinced he was botched, that there was something wrong with him, I remembered how Funes called himself a fragment of a star gone wrong. I wished I could tell him how brave he was, that his thoughts weren't ugly, that I wished I was as brave as him. Then I remembered the wounded red bird that was his heart. And how, for a split second in my dream, its small eye had met my eye—dark, comprehending.

Looking back, I was fooling myself to think I could sneak into Dehaene's old office without anyone noticing. There were surveillance cameras everywhere, it was impossible they wouldn't catch me. Deep down I must have known this. But I was desperate and ignored what I knew. Within weeks I was assigned to the white room—I was to spend my days there. At first I thought maybe this would give some point to my existence. The room was very large and almost empty. There were three white workstations many yards apart that looked like library carrells and each was equipped with a computer and headphones. My only task was to look up whatever I wanted. There was no further explanation. Each morning, sensors were attached to my head and chest; in the late afternoons they were removed. At the rear of the room there was a one-way mirror. Sometimes at the end of the day, I was taken to another room and placed on a gurney that slid into a tunnel-like machine.

I started to wonder if maybe I wasn't botched after all, though in my deepest heart I knew I was.

To this day I don't know if the things I looked up were really of my choosing, or if I was being guided, but without my knowledge. I didn't realize algorithms can lead you from one topic to another without your suspecting you're being lead—you just think you're making choices. If I paused three seconds longer at one site, did the algorithm use that information to reconfigure the search engine, leading me to where the lab wanted me to go? After all, even here in the outside world, there's almost no privacy left anymore. The idea of free choice is muddled, obsolete, corrupted. So why should I have had it there? Still, in those hours I felt almost free. Though I was afraid of what the sensors attached to my head might reveal of me without my knowing.

Even though I knew I shouldn't, a few times I still slipped into Dehaene's old office.

One night, I came across a note in red ink:

"In the near future, mind-reading will be as easy and available as reading from a page."

On the note's other side, also in red ink, was a quote from Proust: "A person is a shadow that can never be penetrated, and of which there can be no such thing as direct knowledge. M. Proust."

The handwriting was Dehaene's. I wondered if he was arguing with himself.

After a few days at my workstation, I was confident I could look up anything I wanted. But when I typed in NeuroSpin, *nothing came up. There was* MIND, Inria, Neurodiderot *("No information is available for this page. Learn why"), and other similar places and names, but not the one I wanted.*

I started to feel almost unreal. Maybe I didn't exist after all, maybe none of it did. The whole room as if floating.

It was like gravity dissolving.

Looking back, I suppose NeuroSpin put blocks on the computer.

Since I couldn't look up NeuroSpin, I looked up Dehaene. It wasn't that I thought he'd be a clue to my predicament, I reminded myself he had left. But with almost no contact with anyone living, his old office made him real to me.

A site said he was Director of INSERM's Cognitive Neuroimaging Unit 52. (There was no mention of NeuroSpin.)

There was a series of quotes. He said the mind blinks like the eye, that a self is a data base dependent on social experiences, and prone to glaring gaps, delusions, misunderstandings.

"Often perceptual decisions are revised to fit the judgment of others, even when that judgment is glaringly incorrect."

He compared the brain to an astronomer watching for supernovae. Just as the news from distant stars takes millions of years to reach us, the information we attribute to the present is outdated by at least one-third of a second.

Another site listed his experiments:

A fetus is attracted to three dots of light arranged in the shape of a face, but hardly at all to three dots shaped like a pyramid.

A nine month-old infant easily acquires phonemes from another human being, but none whatsoever from a video even of the highest quality.

Finally, I came to this: "We are experiencing a revolution. Now, for the first time, all our brain circuits can be repurposed."

That night I lay awake for a long time, turning over the idea of the repurposed brain circuits. Could that have anything to do with me and my several operations? Was there some way it might be relevant to the Empathy Project? As I lay in the darkness, my mind was a smaller, blinder darkness, hemmed in and narrow, the night vast and unknowing.

And so the days in the white room went on.

Often I spent hours hunting down key words: biological, mind, loneliness etc.

"The line between the biological and technological world is exceedingly thin and always unstable." (That felt like a description of myself.)

"Despite technologies that make us more 'connected,' Western industrialized societies are experiencing an epidemic of loneliness and social isolation."

As the weeks drew on, I grew more trepidatious. There was still no explanation of the Empathy Project, or why I was sitting all day at the computer.

Often I felt like a ghost as I read.

"It can be said the Lepton is a lonely particle. Elusive and withdrawn, it does not respond to strong forces." (This was from paragraph 3, page 59, of Formation and Evolution of Galaxies and Large Structures in the Universe, *edited by J. Audouze and J.T.T. Van.)*

I had asked myself, what is an "I", but not what is a "person." But the longer I sat at the computer, the more I understood this also is a question.

Are forests persons? Are dogs and icebergs and deserts persons? Do all existing entities have a right not to be harmed, a right to basic protections? What does it even mean to be "alive"?

Why speak of human rights, not persons' rights?

India acknowledges the legal rights of waterfalls, and in 2017, the New Zealand Parliament granted legal rights to the Whanganui River. When the Genesis Energy Company infringed on its rights, a legal guardian was appointed to defend the river in court. All this I learned from The German Law Journal, Vol. 18 No. 05.

In 2003, the artist Eduardo Kac mixed his DNA with the DNA of a petunia to create the flower-like being, Edunia. Though her appearance was a flower, she was also partly human. He called her a plantimal. Like me, she wasn't just one thing.

The longer I thought about it, the more human beings seemed no more important than any other life-form on Earth.

"All nouns are lonely. They are like crystals enclosing their own little piece of knowledge about the world."

Even Eduardo Kac's Edunia, with her lovingly mixed DNA, seemed lonely. In all the world, there was no other of her kind.

By then, I noticed each time I emerged from the tunnel-like machine, my feelings were a few shades duller than the time before.

But even then, my anxiety was growing. I felt increasingly ghost-like, fragile.

I didn't know who I was or why I was living.

I was more certain than ever I was a failed experiment, and dreaded whatever might come next.

As the cyborg told his lonely story, I pictured him in front of his computer screen, trying to make sense of the life he had been given—a life built on the ruins of his life that had been taken away. A life he couldn't remember.

I wished I could tell him about Georg Cantor's lonely love of infinity, and of Karl Schwarzschild in his trench solving Einstein's equations. Of Funes' heartbeats next to mine but then they vanished. I wished I could tell him of Funes' love for the passionflower.

And I wished I could tell him, too, that he was right to keep speaking, that his story, though sad, companioned me as he hoped it would. I couldn't imagine my life in the emptiness without him.

But each time I tried to speak, no sound came out.

As if part of me was like Funes who had drifted away and was lost forever.

One morning I looked up the word, loneliness.

"Dejected by the awareness of being alone." "Without others of a similar kind, solitary."

The more I looked into it, the more it seemed to infuse the entire world. There were lonely mountains, lonely pillows, lonely dragons, lonely cottages, lonely trees, "the unrelieved loneliness of mid-ocean" on just two pages of the O.E.D.

Ruins "woke a lonely echo."

Gray's Elegy spoke of "lonely Contemplation." Milton wrote, "loneliness is the first thing which Gods nam'd not good."

There were "the bowers of mossy loneliness." (Shelley)

Tennyson wrote of the loneliest island "in a lonely sea."

"A lonely wind swept up the pines."

But the more the word appeared accompanied by its many nouns, the less desolate it started to seem. Almost more like a couple or constellation than a single star.

So if lonely wasn't the word for what I felt, what was? It was a word that needed distance in it, but also dread and loss, bafflement, wonder, violation. And tenderness too, and awe and sorrow.

I had no word for what it was.

Each day the wordless place grew stronger.

Again I pictured the Cyborg at his workstation, alone and afraid of what was coming. The hurt that hurled me from the world had been invisible and left no mark, but every day he faced the signs of his own damage. I remembered how Sister Gudrun said *each brain is embedded in a world of other brains so it seems impossible there should be so much aloneness, but there is*. But the Cyborg's loneliness was even worse—whatever his brain originally was, was lost to him, and yet the feeling of who he had once been persisted. I wished I could go to him, that I could lie down beside him in the dark.

The next word I searched was cyborg.

I soon found it was coined by Manfred E. Clynes and Nathan S. Kline in their landmark paper, Cyborgs and Space, *delivered at the Psychophysiological Aspects of Space Flight Symposium in San Antonio, Texas in 1960.*

I hadn't realized the word was so new, less than a century old. It was a strange feeling to think that for most of history, the word for what I am, what I was made into, didn't even exist.

In restrospect, it makes sense it happened with the movement into outer space. No one had ever been to the moon. Clynes and Kline were considering what adaptations would be necessary for the human body to function beyond gravity. They decided you could approach the problem in one of two ways –alter the human space traveler or alter the environment, and concluded the first option was more practical, also more exciting: "Space travel invites mankind to be proactive in our biological evolution." Scientific advances would permit humankind to expand into alien environments.

They said a human space traveler is "an organism with enhanced abilities due to the integration of one or more technological components, usually involving some aspect of feedback."

But they had completed their entire paper without a term for the new kind of human they envisioned. Where the word would be inserted, they'd left only blanks. With the deadline arriving, they parted, exhausted, for the weekend, no hint of the new word in sight. That weekend Clynes wrackd his brain until suddenly cyborg *emerged and he excitedly phoned Kline to run it by him. Kline said it sounded like a town in Denmark and Clynes agreed but asked him could they use it anyway.*

I had found a small piece of my history.

Over the next days I read about Karl Capek who coined the word robot *from the Czech word for hard, menial labor.*

And I read of how Gregory Bateson asked, is a blind man's cane part of a blind man?

Norbert Weiner believed the boundaries of the human are constructed not innate.

New kinds of bodies lead to new thoughts.

I found sites on embodied computers, cyberspace, dislocation, the intense fear of the other. There were disrupted categories and flows of information.

"No longer confined to the biological skin-bag, we are becoming an extended cognitive architecture whose boundaries far exceed the human body."

"With the invention of cognitive technology, the human brain has reshaped and expanded the space of human reason."

I watched videos of Neil Harbison and Moon Ribas explaining their cyborg identities and advocating for transpecies rights.

But I still couldn't figure out what any of this could have to do with empathy. (Nothing I had been exposed to in the lab lead in the direction of this feeling.) Or how empathy and cyborgs might converge.

By then I was pretty much convinced the lab knew everything about my night-trips to Dehaene's old office. Since being assigned to the white room, I tried to stay away and mostly succeeded. But going there still seemed my only chance to find something out.

I promised myself I would be more efficient. Would make it very quick, stay only a few minutes.

That night to my surprise I found an unlocked file drawer. Lifting out a thin manilla envelope stamped in red ink, I saw the date was several months after Dehaene's departure. Inside, there was a single sheet of paper. I took it with me.

The top of the page read: notes for cyborg memo #1.

This was followed by a series of key points:

• *The cyborg does not have to be problematic. It does not have to be monstrous or deformed.*

• *Pure humanity has always been an illusion. The cyborg collapses conventional binary terms of difference.*

• *The end goal is a highly capable, unfrightening hybrid being.*

• *Texts and sources to be discussed:* The Human Use of Human Beings, The Origins of Feedback Control, Posthumous Bodies, Theories and Applications of Cellular Automata, The Reinvention of Nature.

The remainder of the page was blank.

Maybe I had finally found something relevant. Could this be the memo behind the Empathy Project? A kind of seed?

My mind kept drifting back to "It does not have to be monstrous or deformed." That "it" felt like a knife inside me.

I supposed I wasn't strictly human anymore, but I also wasn't a machine. Why had the whites of my eyes turned gray? Why was one hand slightly larger than another? Why the red scar down my cheek, the black box behind my ear?

Was there a file on me in some office somehere? If there was, I was sure I'd never find it.

The next night when I went back to Dehaene's old office, the door was ajar, the room completely empty. Even the steel bookcase was gone, the holes where it attached to the wall newly filled and painted over.

All I had was the brief, stolen memo.

When I looked at it again, I noticed faint writing on the other side so lightly penciled it was almost impossible to read. Going slowly, I pieced most of it together:

Memo on Human Enhancement and the Future of Warfare

•*In situations of significant uncertainty requiring judgment and knowledge, humans are on the whole superior to computers.*

•*This superiority includes cognitive flexibility and interpretive capacity.*

•*AI is an intrinsically* brittle *system.*

•*AI is central to modern warfare—drones etc.—but there remains an essential role for human combatants.*

•*Optimal military performance requires enhanced strength and neutralized deficits.*

•*The future lies in a human-computer interface; a hybrid combatant.*

At the bottom of the page were the words empathy project. *Three question marks followed.*

I had the two memos, but I was still mostly in the dark. I kept trying to figure out if the memos had anything to do with me. I wasn't a soldier, I was hardly a "highly capable being." And what could empathy and warfare have to do with each other?

Gradually the eerie feeling crept into me that my existence signaled a new world where the boundary between human and machine, animate and inanimate, owner and thing, even between passive and active, was quickly coming to an end. I was a kind of death-knell. But maybe I was also a kind of new beginning—I couldn't decide if this was true.

The more I read about cyborgs, the more I noticed for every positive trait, many more negative, or worse, were mentioned. Cyborgs were the "death of vulnerability, modesty, proportion." They were feared, mistrusted. They were opaque, the unknown, the "other."

But the memo referred to a "highly capable and unfrightening being." So what was I to make of that?

Whatever picture I came up with, I didn't fit inside it.

In the lonely darkness of my mind, I grieved for what I was.

And then one morning, without realizing at first what I was seeing, I came upon the DARPA website. Right away, I scrolled down the list of topics: Military transhumanism. Merging human soldiers and machines. Augmented Cognition. Biohybrids. Brain chip Programs. Neural implants and electrodes. Neural-interface microsystems in relation to emotions.

For each topic there were links to declassified reports, press releases, related projects.

Maybe this would bring me closer to what I was seeking.

Fairly quickly I found this:

DARPA

DEFENSE ADVANCED RESEARCH PROJECTS AGENCY
ENGINEERING HUMANS FOR WAR

Preliminary Report
BMI-303
May 31, 2010

The new frontier of the Defense Sciences is to be found in military-based transhumanism—the notion that man can alter the human condition fundamentally by augmenting and altering the human body with machines and other technologies. As former Director Michael Goldblatt explained at the initiative's inception in 1990, "Soldiers having no physical, physiological, or cognitive limitation will be key to operational dominance and survival."

As part of this effort, we have established the Brain-Machine Interface Project for the study of how brain implants can enhance cognitive ability. One objective of this effort is to develop the use of remote teleoperation via direct interconnections with the brain. The more far-reaching objective is to enable future soldiers to communicate by thought alone. We are envisioning a time when the human brain has its own wireless modem so that instead of acting on thoughts, warfighters have thoughts that act.

In our initial experiments, a chip implanted in a rat's brain enabled the remote-control of the animal's movements. As the project's lead scientist, Eric Eisenstadt, explains, "At first we moved forward very slowly, mindful of potentially complicating circumstances. For instance, might an adversary use this new brain technology to achieve remote guidance or control of our soldiers?" Former Director Goldblatt has struck a reassuring note, "Is having a cochlear implant that helps the deaf hear significantly different from having a chip in the brain controlling thoughts? There are unintended consequences for everything involved in progress that have to be dealt with but cannot be avoided."

In addition to the brain implant project, another key initiative is the Tactical Assault Light Operator Suit which is programmed by a computer chip embedded in the soldier's dog tag. The suit is engineered with embedded sensors, integrated heating and cooling systems, antennas and computers, 3D audio, optics for vision and various light conditions, and, importantly, hemorrhage controls.

Further projects include: The Persistence in Combat project which is currently developing a pain vaccine to limit initial wound-pain to 10-30 seconds, followed by an absence of pain for 30 days. According to Former Director Goldblatt, "This path-breaking vaccine will allow the warfighter to continue on the battlefield as long as bleeding can be controlled. To this end, we are also developing new ways to inhibit bleeding. Our most promising advancement involves the injection of millions of microscopic magnets into each combatant's body so if the need arises, with the mere wave of a wand they can be pulled together as a group to the effected site to stop the bleeding."

In short, through the use of neuromodulation, implantable neural interfaces, neural-interface microsystems, wireless communication with external modules, and other technologies that reliably extract and implant information, as well as enhancements that protect and improve the strength and integrity of the warfighter's body, the important task of engineering humans for war has made—and continues to make—substantial progress.

Even though I'd been operated on several times and remembered nothing of my former life, and was an experimental subject without rights, what I read still shocked me. It was one thing for it to happen to me, but another for some version to be planned for millions of others. And all for the supposed good of humankind, of progress. Could former Director Goldblatt truly believe a cochlear implant and mind control are essentially the same thing? My mind kept spinning.

My eyelids felt leaden. The light from the screen hurt my eyes. I didn't want to see anything.

That night and the next I barely slept. Former Director Goldblatt's comments festered like a poison arrow in my brain: "Soldiers having no physiological or cognitive limitation will be key to survival and operational dominance." "Is having a cochlear implant that helps the deaf hear significantly different from having a chip in the brain controlling thoughts?" I had stumbled into a realm where the drive for mind-control was as real and basic as the sun. And that mind control was linked to military dominance.

I touched the scar on my face, the black box behind my ear, my patchwork skull.

Now that I'd found the DARPA website, I went back to it often. (Those first days when I saw you in the courtyard, I never imagined I'd be telling you these things. I never thought I would tell anyone.) I had the sense I was pointed in the right direction, but I also felt I had a blind spot—that there was something I still couldn't see.

One afternoon I went through the lists of DARPA projects. It seemed there was nothing too outlandish to pursue. (Part of me admired their boldness, while another part recoiled.)

There was the μBRAIN Project that was developing prototype biological models from miniature insects. "Nature has forced on these small creatures a drastic compactness and energy efficiency; with no more than a few hundred neurons they maintain basic functionality. Mapped onto suitable hardware, their impressive functioning can be transferred to humans."

MOANA was dedicated to "the use of light to make possible brain to brain communication."

There was also a list of DARPA's outstanding past inventions: the computer mouse (1964), the GPS (1983), Drones (1988) and the proto-internet, Arpanet (1969).

There were many more pages of new ones under development:

Exacto Bullets control their own trajectories, altering and correcting their flight-paths in mid-flight. Geckskin is a high-grip synthetic named after the Gecko lizard that will enable a human being to easily scale a glass wall. LS3 is a robotic pack animal that functions on the battlefield as a beast of burden. The Solar Eagle drone with its a wing-span equivalent to a 40-story building will stay airborne for as long as five years.

My mind filled with these new projects and inventions. But I still hadn't found the link to empathy. My blind spot was strong. What wasn't I seeing?

I pictured the Cyborg in the white room, hunched and effortful as he tried to make sense of who he was and what was being asked of him. How as he read, the world grew more bizarre, more threatening. And more ingenious, twisted, rapt, haunted. More remote, yet in certain ways closer. And how he spoke of it to no one.

Sister Gudrun called me a prodigy, but the more the Cyborg spoke, it was clear I knew almost nothing.

I thought back to him standing under the oak tree, and how, the whole time he was there, I never even sensed his presence. In my blindness, I had believed I was completely alone.

He had been homeless and thirsty but he stayed nearby and felt me sicken.

He was an orphan planet spinning in its caul of ice. A lost passionflower. A hybrid like Edunia.

And he was none of those things.

He was an experimental subject, and he was alone.

I was learning about cyborgs and warfare, but not empathy. I decided to look it up. Maybe that would help me find the link I was missing.

"Empathy is the ability to understand and share the feelings of another... the vicarious experiencing of the feelings, thoughts, or attitudes of another."

"In neuroscience it is defined as any process where the attended perception of the object's state generates a state in the subject that is more applicable to the object's state or situation than to the subject's own prior state or situation. This capacity evolved with the mammalian brain, particularly the thalamocingulate division of the forebrain."

Then I came to: "Empathy paves the way for moral reasoning and inhibits aggression."

I read that sentence twice. Something deep inside me paused and listened. That night I dreamed again about black holes. Their fierce emptiness shining. I watched two merge—liquid, dark—two vortexes melding into one deeper, stronger vortex. And as I watched, this sentence came back into my mind, "Empathy paves the way for moral reasoning and inhibits aggression." And then another thought rose through the dream—If empathy inhibits aggression, isn't it counterproductive for military operations.

I opened my eyes. The room was still dark. My thoughts moved like liquid mercury inside me—shining and slipping. Gradually they came more into focus: DARPA was pursuing the hybridization of humans for warfare. In order to create super-effective combatants and occupying forces, wouldn't it make sense to rid them of all empathetic responses, much like ridding their bodies of bleeding wounds or vulnerability to infection.

I thought back to the tunnel-like machine. It dulled my feelings. Could that have something to do with what I was now wondering?

If the lab's goal was to make an unfeeling hybrid being, they'd failed miserably with me. And since that was the case, why was I still with them, why hadn't they gotten rid of me?

Over the next days I learned more about empathy.

A bonobo witnessing a bonobo in distress seeks out more bodily comfort than if the distressing event were happening to itself.

A rat will willingly forgo a delicious treat in order to help out another rat.

Voles console their fearful partners.

Chimps apply healing insects to the wounds of other chimps.

In a lab experiment, a macaque went hungry for two weeks rather than pull a chain that would release its food but physically harm another macaque.

When the conservationist Lawrence Anthony died suddenly of a heart attack on March 2, 2012, a group of elephants traveled to his home on the edge of the reserve and stood vigil for several nights.

By the age of 12 months, a human infant will try to comfort a person in distress.

I closed my eyes. The room swayed like a fragile wing in darkness.

"Research suggests a gene located near LRRN1 on chromosome 3 controls the human ability to understand and respond to the emotions of others."

"fMRI imaging shows the involvement of a complex empathetic network distributed across the brain's superior temporal sulcus, insula, and medial and orbital cortices. Additional involvement is found in the amygdala and anterior cingulate cortex, as well as in a variety of autonomic and neuroendocrine processes."

I had the two memos and DARPA's Preliminary Report BMI-303: Engineering Humans for War. *I had the name of the project I was part of, the Empathy Project, but no description. I decided it seemed likely I was right—the lab was in search of a highly efficient hybrid warrior undeterred by empathy.*

I was as far from an efficient warrior as anyone could imagine. I wondered again why the lab would keep me.

Unsure what to type next, I just tried out various things—grief, gravity, war, bonobos, biocybernetics.

Through a series of clicks I can no longer remember, I ended up at Manfred Clynes again, the man who coined the word "cyborg." He was referencing his early paper, "The Biocybernetics of Emotion," which interrogated the fundamentals of human feeling, and was solicited and then rejected by the Journal of Astronautics *in 1973. (He said most of his peers dismissed his interest in emotions as trivial, weird, off-putting.). As I read the excerpts, I found them oddly moving.*

"Because we are inhabitants of Earth, our dreams and emotions, our in-out tidal flow of breath, our most intimate gestures, are tied to the strength and direction of gravity. But what happens when we leave the planet and move beyond our gravitational home? Without gravity, will joy feel the same or different? What is it about grief that ties it to heaviness? How will grief feel without any outer heaviness when we are weightless?"

"How do our most intimate emotions arrive at the shapes and gestures that express them?"

"In the future, when we have relocated to outer space, will we experience the same emotions as on Earth, or others that we don't yet know exist?"

I felt like I could feel him thinking. That the questions he asked were beautiful the way anything striving and vulnerable is beautiful.

I had been operated on, modified, tampered with, implanted with devices I wasn't told about and didn't understand. I had been changed irrevocably. And yet, as Clynes implied, there are still so many ways I, or anyone, can be altered even further—not only by human intervention but by change of circumstance, environment. I had wanted to think there is a borderline between a self and the world, between a body and the world, even if that line is porous. But that line was dissolving.

"The machine-like self is born of our aggression toward our emotional and bodily limitations. In the image of the cyborg we deny our dependency upon nature and our own most vulnerable human qualities, our frailty and limitations."

Everywhere I looked there were more thoughts to consider.

"Technology is made by humans. If we modify our bodies with human creations we become more human."

"Life will be much more exciting when we turn from creating applications for mobile phones and start creating them for our own bodies."

"When we extend our senses, we extend our knowledge."

"Cars can now detect if something is behind them, but humans still lack this ability. Why are we giving this ability to a car when we could give it to ourselves?"

The more I read, the more lonely I began to feel, set adrift in a sea of ideas where I tried to find myself but couldn't.

"The use of cyborgs in industry will lead to vast unemployment and widespread economic hardship and discrimination."

"Bodies are information channels."

"The body becomes a hyperpragmatic prosthesis in a world of virtual realities."

The artificial liver research of Yukhiko Nose, Michio Mito, and Morokazu Hori in early 1956 was referred to as "a dreamful challenge."

But I didn't feel like a "dreamful challenge." I didn't know how to think about what I really was.

At night as I lay in the darkness, my uneasiness deepened.

By then I was sleeping very little. Each day at the computer, my exhausted fingers moved clumsily over the keyboard. The air was oscillating filaments of light that swam like schools of minnows.

So when Deadpool came up on the screen, I didn't know what I had done, how it happened.

All I saw was his masked face, and underneath, a caption:

"When the mercenary Deadpool fell ill with an uncontrollable terminal cancer, he reluctantly agreed to undergo secret treatments by Weapon X as part of their experimental bio-enhancement program. Though the treatments saved his life, they sent his immune system into over-drive and left him badly disfigured with scars and fresh lesions brought on by excessive cell regeneration."

I had never heard of Deadpool, didn't know a single thing about him. I rested my head on the workstation's flat surface. It was hard to take it all in. I just wanted to rest, but behind my closed eyes I saw Deadpool's face—the lesions oozing like infected branches, his dark shame at what he had become. But his eyes were different, they were filled with a clear and quiet understanding.

Sometimes he wiped his weeping sores, but nothing he could do could dry them.

The next day at my workstation, I flipped from one mindless video to another—I can't even remember what they were. Maybe cooking shows, pet tricks, K Pop. Things like that. I didn't want to try anymore, just wanted to drift away in my mind. Why didn't they just get rid of me? Why did I still go to the white room?

Minnows of light shimmered in the air before me.

The night was cold. Sleepless as usual, I glanced down at my misshapen hand, the skin's odd sheen, when from the corner of my eye I noticed a blurred shape in the doorway. It was moving toward me. As it drew closer, I realized it was Deadpool.

Standing beside me, he peeled back his mask. Lesions like wads of moist chewing gum covered his face. They were a color like old brick but also different, dull and bright at the same time. One crimson z-shaped lesion festered along his right cheek.

I told myself I must be dreaming, but I knew I wasn't.

There was something dignified, almost sad, in how he held himself—purposeful and calm at the same time. As if balancing a glass vial on each shoulder.

As if movement and thought were the same thing.

After a few seconds he returned the mask to his face and looked into my eyes and spoke. "It's true Weapon X's healing factor allowed me to live, but as soon as the treatments were completed, I sensed right away whatever they'd done to me, more than my immune system was effected. I suspected they'd done more than they claimed or would ever admit. When I tried to remember my childhood, I couldn't. I forgot many other things as well. Over the next days, sometimes it seemed my memories came back, but each time they kept changing, so I knew they hadn't. The rapid cell regeneration had destabilized my brain. I didn't know if this was an accident or planned by Weapon X. I felt almost no emotion.

Imagine a desert of pale sand. The sun scorches it and the nights lay down their mild coolness, but the sand feels nothing. That's what I was like.

And yet beneath the muted feelings, something in me was agitated, mournful, erratic. I sensed, but didn't know, who I was. I fell into fits of rage and despair.

Was my real name Wade Wilson or had I stolen it from someone else? Did my father die in a bar room brawl or had he lived a long life of military service? Did he treat me with kindness or was I beaten and abused? Sometimes I was certain my mother died when I was five, at other times I remembered my teenage self with her standing beside me.

After a few months, pieces of my life came back. I knew I worked as a mercenary and had traveled all over the globe—maybe that's why I know so many languages—Japanese, German, Spanish, ASL. To this day, like you, I live partly in conjecture.

When I regained strength enough to think things through for more than a few minutes, I wondered what Weapon X was after. Why did they bother to save me? What was in it for them? And in their eyes, was my outcome a success or failure? Or maybe both?

Once it was clear I would go on living, I asked myself these questions."

Then as quietly as he came to me, he left me.

Why had he come to me? He didn't say and I didn't think to ask. Was he real or unreal? I was sure he wasn't a dream, but I also knew my certainty made no sense. If he wasn't a dream, what else could he be?

All I knew was when he stood beside me, something in me paused and opened.

After a while I stopped asking myself if he was real. I knew he was but also that it made no sense and I could never prove it.

The only hint of why he came to me, if it even was a hint at all, was that he said, "Like you, I live partly in conjecture." From that one comment, it seemed plausible he knew who I was. But beyond that I knew nothing.

(If Deadpool had never come to me, I probably never would have come to you. Wouldn't have been brave enough or even understood that it could matter. He was the only being who had ever addressed me as a person.)

After that first night, he returned many times, and each time, whatever he told me, I just wanted to listen. And though he came without warning, I never felt any reason to fear him.

That next day when he returned, he explained more about Weapon X:

"The Weapon X compound was divided into two main sections—Section K, where the clandestine biological experiments were carried out, and the Workshop, also known as the Hospice, where the failed experimental subjects were sent and locked up—it was basically a prison. Since most of the experiments failed, the Workshop was full to overflowing.

Weapon X was involved in biological enhancement in every form and from every angle you could think of. Its earliest focus was on standard genetic engineering—altering and manipulating gene expression with an aim toward creating super-enhanced soldiers and assassins—but over time the experiments turned increasingly outlandish, even grotesque. No method or outcome was too perverse or violent. They were willing to try anything.

A few months after my bio enhancement, it became clear Weapon X considered me part-success, part-failure. The treatments had stopped the cancer, but my skin was messed up, my behavior erratic. At least that's how they saw it.

Considering my skin and other failings, I expected they'd send me to the Hospice. Weapon X's initial hope for me(I learned this later) was I'd carry out their riskiest, most complex and treacherous covert operations, but the way I turned out, they didn't trust me. To my surprise, at least for a while, they decided to use me anyway."

Each time Deadpool came, he entered so quietly I didn't hear him. I'd just look up and there he was, standing beside me. As soon as I saw him, my heart calmed, my mind turned almost peaceful. (I had mostly stopped wondering what he was—a real being, a dream, an apparition. My wondering seemed a wrong language. Those categories dissolved inside me.)

Soon, it occurred to me the face he was looking at—my face—was a face I'd never seen. (The computer screen was non-reflective.) So of the two faces in the room, his was hidden behind a mask, and in a sense mine was too—I'd never seen it—but mine was a kind of one-way mask that left me invisible to myself but visible to Deadpool. There was something peaceful in being seen. It was like looking up at the night sky, the constellations. How they are simply there, always have been.

That second night, when he came back, he told me more about Weapon X:

"They were going to send me out into the world, but not yet, they said I wasn't ready. I was still exhausted from the treatments, from whatever they had done to me. In truth, I was worse than they knew. Time had become strange to me. Very often the past and future slid back and forth inside the present, and sometimes the present suddenly caught fire. I stood there in the raging flames. I kept this to myself.

In my confinement, I spent hours every day in the Section K library. Above its door was an inscription: Cyborgs are the life-blood and heartbeat of our new world.

I decided to look up others of my kind. Who were they? How did they live? Were they like me or different?

I'd probably known all this before, but in my newly-damaged memory it was lost. I wanted to try to bring it back.

Right away I saw there are endless routes and forms of transformation. I made a list.

Cable was infected as an infant with a techno-organic virus that altered his basic cellular structure. He reconfigures his body parts at will, shifting between the mechanical and organic.

As a child, Ivan was stricken with an incurable illness. His father, a famous brain surgeon, couldn't save him but performed an operation that endowed him with extrasensory powers.

The ballet dancer, Francoise, can see through objects and walls.

Albert's hands turn into razors.

Pyunma is a soldier horrified at his fish-like body, with his mechanical lungs and silver scales. No matter how hard he tries, he can't adjust to what he has become.

There are whole bands of children with bodies that are armored weapons.

Vision's consciousness is derived from encephalograms of a dead man's brain.

The captive, Ladytron, was rebuilt with robotic parts and turned into an unwilling assassin.

After a horrific accident, Steele's brain was transplanted into a robotic body. He is consumed with a longing to be human.

The brilliant pacifist scientist, Michael Collins, was reconfigured against his will and turned into a living weapon of mass destruction.

This last one may have distressed me the most."

After Deadpool recited his mostly terrible list, he fell silent. I thought about Ladytron, Michael Collins, the others. Of the unforgivable violation. How like them I had been tampered with until the self I knew was gone from me and I'd been left some sort of hybrid of myself and something else, something other. For so long I had blamed myself, felt the shame of it but not the violation. But now, as I thought of them, I added myself to their list. My temples pounding, I fell into a dreamless sleep.

Some nights I still dreamed:

I was in a desert with Deadpool. The noon sun beat down, we were weak and thirsty, our cracked lips dry as sand. Deadpool was still wearing his mask and bodysuit, he couldn't bring himself to take them off. We were exhausted but didn't know where to head next. For a long time, we fell quiet. Then all of a sudden Deadpool started singing. It was a beautiful song—strange and slow and tender, and he sang it for many hours.

When I woke, his voice was a soft wind inside me.

Although I got used to him coming, I never knew what Deadpool would say next. It was like standing at the ocean's edge, not knowing if you'd see a fin or spout or bottle or broken shell or something much weirder, beyond identity or comprehension. I liked the not-knowing. My questions and blindnesses were slender threads that bound me to him, fragilely and lightly. And as much as I'd grown used to him coming, I was always aware he might never come back.

One day as he stood beside me he said this:

"What is power?" I didn't know if he wanted me to think of an answer, or wait for him to tell me. (But of course, like you, I never spoke.) Then slowly he turned to me, and slowly he continued:

"For many months after I left the Weapon X compound, I carried out all sorts of covert operations, took on the most dangerous assignments. But always I lived with the threat my illness could come back. That it could happen at any moment. So although my appearance was powerful, what power did I really have? If the healing factor failed, I'd be sent to Hospice with the others.

My so-called power was a house of mirrors.

By then I'd noticed cyborgs in books and movies are treated with grudging ambivalence at best. On the one hand, our enhanced powers can be seen as useful, even admired, but on the other hand, we are suspect and frightening—who can really trust us?—at any second we might turn against the human race. That's when it occurred to me that although at first it appears what makes us frightening is our potential for angry, destructive, uncontrollable power, really the opposite is true: it's our powerlessness that frightens humans most—the idea that just as once we were transformed against our will, the same could happen to them. What's been done to us could be done to anyone. Who can believe themselves safe from suddenly being strapped down, injected, operated on, whatever—from becoming a body without agency or rights. From becoming an "other" like us. Isn't this what haunts the human soul?—

What happened to us could just as easily happen to them. And once it happens, you can't change yourself back.

Is Ladytron powerful? Is Steele? Is the pacifist Michael Collins powerful?

I was healed but what did that mean?

Many nights I walked beneath the winter stars and hardly knew who I was."

As I listened, it felt so strange to think that before the Cyborg ever knew me, much like the way he would come to me, Deadpool had already come to him. And when Deadpool stepped from the shadows, the Cyborg felt, like I did, grateful, less alone. The fragile thread he spoke of connecting him to Deadpool was like the invisible silken thread I felt with him—tenuous and wild, unbroken. And the question of what is real, hadn't I let go of that too? No words were the right words.

I never asked myself why Deadpool wanted to tell me his story. I never wondered if it was for me or him or for us both. In a way it seemed less a story than a part of nature, and I listened to it the way you listen to the rain, the way it just comes down. You listen and then suddenly it stops and there is sun.

Sometimes he stood so close I could feel the air warming in the space between our bodies.

"The cancer was gone, I was out in the world again working for Weapon X, running missions for covert operations. It helped keep my mind off my grotesque, oozing body.

As it turned out, my new blood was highly resistant to chemicals and poisons. And as a marksman, I was even quicker and more accurate than before. Whatever I set out to do, I did it better than ever. A large faction at Weapon X had written me off as little more than medical waste, a miscarriage of science and technology—disfigured, brainsick, erratic—given how I performed, I thought maybe now they'd reconsider.

But after a few months, the treatment started failing. The cancer had come back.

I knew if Weapon X found out they'd force me into treatment or lock me up in Hospice, or both.

That's when the strange sensations began. I'd almost forgotten what it's like to be a feeling being. But gradually over a few days my feelings came back to me. And the odd thing was, they were more vivid and complex than before.

It was like the difference between seeing from a distance and seeing up close.

I had been a desert, and now where there'd been only rocks and sand, wildflowers were growing. They were exquisite and small and I wanted to be near them. Wanted, almost, to protect them. They seemed almost to have faces. Before this, any mention of flowers would have struck me as absurd and girlish. But these were different. They had meaning. They were soft and strong and understood many things.

I began wandering random streets for hours at a time. Nothing I came across lacked dignity or purpose. Nothing was too small or insubstantial. No shred of garbage, scrap metal, frayed string.

My bones were aching. Soon I was too weak to walk without a cane. But every day I kept walking.

Colors astonished me. I hadn't known there were so many—several thousands, at least. Each with its own specific feeling. I only wanted to be with them, and with all the sounds that also came and went, the many kinds of winds and rain, gradations of daylight and dark.

By the time Weapon X tracked me down, I was nearly unconscious. They wheeled me in for another round of treatments.

When I woke, the flowers and pieces of scrap metal were gone. If something in me mourned, I didn't know it. Once again, I felt nothing."

In my mind's eye I saw Deadpool strapped onto the gurney and wheeled in for a new round of treatments. I saw him walking with his cane among the garbage heaps and twisted metal. I saw Ladytron trapped in her robotic body. And Schwarzschild in his trench where something unnameable was happening inside him. I saw the letters on Funes' strip of screen flicker and waver like black flames. They were hurt and lost and beautiful and no matter how close they seemed I couldn't touch them.

The more he came, the more I lived for Deadpool's visits. Whenever he was with me, something deep inside me suddenly made sense. It was hard to hear about his suffering, but even then, his voice was oddly calm and reassuring.

I still spent my days in the white room. I didn't really know what to do there anymore. Any leads I followed just lead to thoughts that they'd get rid of me. That I was botched and useless. Thoughts I didn't want to have.

A few times I looked into areas I knew I shouldn't. I typed in "cyborg injections", "emotionally aware technology", "high-fidelity mind-states," "pros and cons of electronic brains." Then quickly wiped them out.

Each time Deadpool came, his tale grew darker:

"The second round of treatments was complete, but Weapon X wasn't pleased. The result was an improvement over the first, but not to a 'significant degree.' They were tired of my uncontrollable behavior and erratic brain. The decision was made to transfer me to Hospice.

I was still dulled and weak from the treatments. But even in my haze I dreaded what was happening.

Hospice was the last place on Earth I wanted to be. I'd heard all the rumors.

Moonlight crept across the floorboards, and all through the night I planned the escape I was too weak to carry out.

At daybreak, I was strapped onto a stretcher and carried past the outer gate of Section K."

I wondered what Deadpool felt as he spoke, if there was something he wanted from me I didn't give. Or did he want nothing more than my listening—the one thing I gave with all my heart. And I wondered, too, though he never said it, had he come to help me? He knew I was frightened and alone. Though on the surface his story was different from mine, and much more drastic, there were ways it also wasn't. It helped me to hear another like myself, an experimental subject who had been trapped, feeling his way forward.

Deadpool continued: "I was in Hospice. I had been there a few weeks. The lesions on my face were oozing. Bits of lightning flashed inside my hands and chest. My exhaustion was gone, but my brain-cells were buzzing. Frenetic thoughts hurled up all sorts of junk.

Wherever I turned, objects fell apart before my eyes—chairs and tables crumbled into heaps of dust and splinters. Within seconds, a bare tree through the window-bars became covered with white flowers. For hours on end video monitors on the wall looped nothing but my ruined face. For awhile I grew convinced I had been through a terrible conflagration, that my mask and bodysuit had burned and I'd burned with them. I was the ghost of myself, unbodied but still captive. The room had a soundtrack—it was always playing. Or maybe it was several soundtracks at once. Flower-sounds mixed in with the sounds of viruses and exploding planets. There were endless combinations. I heard the electromagnetic structure of matter.

My skin sounded like the winter sun.

Dr. Killebrew's voice came from somewhere nearby. He said there were still ways to alter and enhance me. His aim was to create the perfect biological weapon.

Leather straps secured my wrists. My eyes were burning."

The moment Deadpool mentioned Dr. Killebrew's plan to make a perfect biological weapon, my chest clenched, my throat tightened. That night after he left, I took out the page I'd stolen from Dehaene's old office, read it again. I thought back to the DARPA website. If the operations on me had succeeded, I would have the makings of the perfect hybrid soldier DARPA wanted—undeterred by human feeling. But the operations failed, I'd never been what they wanted. And again I wondered, what happens to a failed experimental subject? Deadpool and the others were sent to Hospice, but what was going to happen to me? Why was the lab keeping me? Why was I still there? Why did I spend my days in the white room? None of it made sense.

That night I dreamed I was in the Hospice with Deadpool. Like him, I wore a bodysuit and mask. All the walls were mirrored. They were like light, but solid, and many objects were magnetized inside them—they didn't drift away. I walked toward one wall and saw myself draw closer. For the first time it would be possible to see my face. I removed the mask. My heart was pounding. But beneath my mask was another mask, moist and oozing. I couldn't know who I was.

When Deadpool came back the next night, his story took an even stranger turn.

"Dr. Killebrew had finished with me for the day, I lay exhausted in a corner of the room. Whatever he had done, it had caused me great pain. The usual soundtrack was on, but something else came through the wall—I realized it was the moans and cries of other experimental subjects. I had never heard them before.

One lesion near my eye was different from the rest; more like a black, silken thread. Distressed, exhausted, I touched it unthinkingly. (Normally I strictly avoided touching my face.) And as soon as I did, an odd thing happened—a small cluster of words came out of it. It's hard to explain what it was like, I didn't exactly see or hear them, I just knew they were there. It was like a combination of seeing and hearing, but different.

The words were mysterious, oddly beautiful: hurt shadows of suppose.

Once again I touched the lesion, and again the word-clusters came: hypnotized by mourning; itself beyond itself; the ruined hand of the dark among the stars."

For a few minutes Deadpool fell silent. Maybe he wanted me to pause at his clusters of words, to feel them as he had. To really stop and take them in. Hurt shadows of suppose moved like a soft wind against my skin. It reminded me of my dream of Deadpool in the desert, singing. How his tender, haunting, song lasted for many hours.

After a few minutes he continued:

"It's not that the word clusters made sense to me, but there was something beautiful in them, and hurt and of the world. Something broken and intact at the same time.

'And flowering with difficulty.' 'And flames in the most secret places.' "The fragile because.'

The nights felt less cold. My mind less lonely."

When he turned to leave, the strange flower of the "fragile because" wavered inside me.

From the earliest days I could remember, my loneliness was a raw, worm-shaped wound inside my heart. A wound I wanted to get rid of. But now I began to wonder if maybe it wasn't such a bad thing after all. Maybe without it the Cyborg would never have come to me. Sister Gudrun once told me people like to think literature was born when a boy ran out of the Neanderthal valley chased by a wolf, but in fact it was born on the day the boy ran out of the valley crying *wolf!* but there was no wolf behind him.

And now, as the Cyborg was repeating the words from Deadpool's lesion—"flowering with difficulty", "the fragile because" I saw Funes' passionflower in the air before me. It had been a long time since I'd seen it. So long since I'd felt Funes' heartbeat. And again I wondered where he had gone to. Was he alive or dead? It seemed he had been dying, but how could I be sure?

For a few days, the Cyborg didn't come back. I didn't know where he was. I didn't want to lose him.

Although Deadpool told me odd, surprising things, he always spoke in a plain, straightforward way. He made them seem just part of the world, facts among countless other facts. Ordinary, blunt. Though often when he spoke, he turned away for a few seconds and looked into the distance:

"From the moment I touched the lesion, my feelings began to come back again. And now that I had them, I resisted Dr. Killebrew. Whenever I touched the lesion, I felt the suffering of my fellow inmates—especially Worm, who had tried to befriend me. There was a holding room where a bunch of us were kept. We started a betting pool, taking bets on who would die first. We called it the Deadpool. (So now you see where I got my name. After I escaped, I took it as my own. It reminded me of my friends in Hospice.) Dr. Killebrew had grown frustrated over his series of failed experiments, and one day, depressed by a new batch of disappointing results, he lobotomized then tortured Worm. As Worm lay suffering on a table, he begged me to kill him and I did—with one swift motion I broke his neck. A hot wave of grief swept through my chest, but none of it showed on my face.

Later that night I escaped.

I walked beneath the vastness of the stars."

Even on the nights when Deadpool didn't come, my room felt less sterile, kinder, almost softer. The shadow of Deadpool's voice moved through it.

Every day I still went to the white room, spent hours in front of the computer, still wondering what I was doing there and why the Empathy Project still hadn't been explained to me. Why mention it at all if they wouldn't explain? I asked myself, how could I be part of something that I had no clue what it was? But of course, in another way I knew the answer—my life didn't belong to me.

One afternoon I looked up "ownership" and "own": "Legal possession of"; "accepting responsibility for, taking control over"; "to acknowledge something to be true or valid."

"Belonging to oneself."

At Weapon X, Deadpool and Worm didn't belong to themselves, though Worm tried to have some say over his dying.

There are so many ways of being enslaved.

I looked down at my hands on the keyboard—who owned them? Though I could make them move, did they belong to me?

Why did the lab have no mirrors? Why had I never seen my face?

That night when Deadpool came back, I was sad and weary. But when I looked into his eyes, something in me opened and turned toward him.

As he spoke, the strange story of his lesion turned even stranger.

"I had been alone most of my life. Had killed artfully and swiftly. Prided myself in the skill with which I did this. But after the words came, I realized I'd been living in a kind of blindness. The words were shining eyes in the darkness, I wanted them to teach me how to see.

By then I had escaped from the Hospice. I knew Weapon X would be looking for me. That's the only thing I knew for certain.

Aloneness is not one thing, it keeps changing.

I didn't know where I was or where I could go. I walked for many days and finally came to an abandoned cabin by a lake. The bare cot inside was all I needed.

My legs were sore, the marks on my face had grown plumper, worm-like, moist. I wondered if they'd spread inside me.

In my weariness I touched the silken lesion. Unlike the other sores it never wept or bled.

But this time, instead of word-clusters, whole sentences came out.

I was dehydrated and tired beyond measure. I thought I must be having a hallucination.

After a while I realized the lesion was telling me a story.

Why would it do this? I was perplexed and exhausted but tried to pay attention.

Stars glittered in the cabin's broken window."

"The story was about a dog named Laika. I closed my eyes in the darkness, felt it wash over me.

After a few sentences, I realized Laika was real, not imaginary, the first dog sent into outer space.

As the lesion's story unfolded, I learned she was one of a group of Moscow street-dogs rounded up for a secret program to send the first canine into space. Data was needed on the effects of space travel on a 'complex biological organism'. Street dogs were chosen because they were 'survivors of the hardships of hunger and bad weather, they'd already proved their toughness.' And all the chosen dogs were female, 'more naturally compliant than males', their small stature also fit the narrow cabin.

'The specimen is a five-kilogram mongrel female, probably part husky, white with brown markings, approximately three years old.'

At the intake center they described her as 'quiet and charming.'

She was quickly evaluated for 'outstanding levels of passivity and obedience' and passed with flying colors.

Only one of the ten canine trainees would be sent into space.

If Laika was chosen for the mission, she would become the first living being to orbit the Earth alone."

That night I couldn't sleep. I thought to myself, I am an experimental subject listening to an experimental subject tell me the life-story of an experimental subject. And I started to realize that being an experimental subject is like being in someone else's dream—but it's a dream you can't wake up from because you are the dream.

My temples ached. Worms of light swam before my eyes. The walls softened.

For months I'd hunted for some sense of who I was and why I existed, but from the moment Deadpool started talking about Laika, something in me slowed and quieted. A small fissure opened. I wondered if Deadpool felt this also.

The next night he continued.

"The lesion released so many words, often it was hard to keep up. I wished it would slow down so I could feel what I was learning. I understood Laika was real, she existed. This made her fate all the more tender and painful. I listened more carefully than I had ever listened to anything:

I learned that during her first hours at the training center, Laika was implanted with sensors for monitoring her biological data. A small loop of her carotid artery was pulled through the flesh of her neck. This would be the attachment point for the biological monitors on Sputnik 2.

Over the next days, she was fitted with a spacesuit and waste receiver. The spacesuit had attachment rings to chain her to the capsule.

I pictured a small dog in a spacesuit, obedient, baffled, then I thought of Worm strapped to his table, how in the end he had no idea what was happening.

But compared to Worm, Laika's suffering was slower, layered."

"Laika's training was extremely rigorous and relentless.

In order to get her used to confinement, she was locked inside progressively smaller pressurized capsules. Her first confinement lasted a few hours, her final one for 20 days. As her isolation grew more prolonged, she learned not to cry.

Other parts of her training included a centrifuge that mimicked the violent acceleration and noises of space flight. Inside it, her heart rate soared, her blood pressure spiked, her respiration quickened. In yet another device, she was secured to a mechanical arm and spun in circles.

In zero gravity, regular dog food flies out of its bowl, so technicians developed a gelatinous mix of agar, water, dried meat and beef fat, which Laika repeatedly refused. But with her regular food withheld from her, she learned to eat it. On a space flight, this mixture would provide the only source of water."

That night after the Cyborg left me I had another dream.

Laika was inside the capsule, looking out its small window. All her trainers had gone home for the night. The room was varying patches of darknesses, some lighter, almost gray, slow dancers moving out of reach. Then she wasn't Laika anymore, but Funes. But how could he fit inside so small a capsule, and where was his cot? He was holding a passionflower in his hand, its petals the purple-black of the night sky, and his eyes were moist with tears. He looked at me but didn't see me. Then I woke.

The Cyborg was back again, Deadpool's story continued:

"By all accounts Laika was highly disciplined, selfless, obedient. Devoted to her caregivers and trainers.

So it wasn't a surprise when after a few weeks, three finalists were chosen and Laika was among them. The other two were Mukha and Albina.

What the scientists knew but didn't say was the technology to return to Earth had not yet been invented. The chosen dog would die in space.

Which one of the final three would they choose?

Mukha was considered too homely to represent the state—her hind legs were too short, her body disproportionate. She was picked as the control, her real-time biological data on Earth would be compared to the real-time data sent back from the canine in space.

Albina was beautiful with silky white hair and perfect proportions, and had already served on several minor missions. The trainers knew and loved her best. 'Albina was everyone's darling. It was exceedingly painful to think of sending her to her death' so Albina was named backup.

Laika was chosen so Albina could live."

"The director of the space program was Sergei Korolev, an army Colonel and engineer—for many years his identity was kept top secret.

Under Stalin, he'd been condemned to seven years of hard labor, dragged from his home in St. Petersburg and shipped off in a boxcar to the gulag at Kolyma, in Siberia. By the time he left there, all his teeth had rotted out, his jaw was broken, his heart muscle damaged. He served the remainder of his sentence in a series of specialized prisons for engineers and scientists.

But now, under his direction, the Soviet space program would achieve the first launch of an artificial Earth satellite, the first launch of a biological satellite, the first uncrewed moon landing, and would send the first human—Yuri Gagarin—into space. Andrei Leonov would perform the first spacewalk.

But there was something curious, even disconcerting about Korolev—almost tender. Despite his high rank and many bureaucratic pressures, every morning when he arrived at work the first thing he did was visit the dogs, and he visited them again every night before he left. It's said he did this without fail, and always checked the temperature of their water, making sure it wasn't too warm."

As Deadpool recounted the lesion's words, I couldn't help but feel baffled at the Colonel's tender-seeming soul.

Could both things be true—that Korolev was a kindly man and former tortured prisoner (the tortured prisoner still alive inside him), but also the bureaucrat presiding over Laika's suffering who insisted she be spun in circles, confined for weeks at a time, and terrorized by loud noises and vibrations. The one who arranged to send her to her death.

Was there a Korolev watching over me and I didn't know it? Someone who was in certain ways kind, who had suffered? But I had no evidence that this was so.

Each night after Deadpool left me, I lay in the darkness and wondered what Laika had been thinking and feeling. How did she make sense of what was done to her, what was happening, how did she explain it without words?

Deadpool's lesion stressed her discipline and patience, her good nature, how she excelled at her tasks and was eager to please.

Whenever a face appeared at the capsule window, she "wagged her tail with canine joy."

Amidst the frightening noises and vibrations, unlike me she bonded with her captors.

Night after night, as I listened to Deadpool recount Laika's story, it was like watching a mud slide in slow motion, or a soldier in the jungle in the few seconds before ambush—you can see his eyes, you know what's coming.

I saw in my mind's eye a photograph Deadpool told me the lesion had described. It was of Laika crouched on a metal table with Korolev half-sitting, half-standing, behind her. With one hand he holds her in place, his hand so large it completely covers her chest. His shirt is striped like a prisoner's, the sleeves rolled up, the collar unbuttoned. Both of them stare directly at the camera. It is a moment that seems like it can last forever, as if whatever threatens her is near but will never inch closer, never reach her.

But then I thought of Deadpool's story about Worm, how time didn't stop for him. The tears welled in my chest.

I could almost feel Laika's brittle ribs. How easy it would be to break them.

The more I listened to the Cyborg, it seemed he and Laika and Funes were almost the same lonely being—the only being I had ever loved. And that where freedom should be, there are chains and attachment rings, injured legs, sealed capsules. But even as they mourned and suffered, something in their hearts still wandered through the wind and stars. This was the one thing I never doubted.

"The weekend before Laika's transfer to the launch site, against all regulations, Vladimir Yazdovsky, the canine program's director, took Laika home with him to enjoy the outdoors and play with his children.

A veteran army surgeon, Yazdovsky was responsible for Laika's daily training.

'I wanted to do something nice for her since she didn't have much longer to live. She was a wonderful dog, quiet and even-tempered. The children were entranced by her serenity and gracious demeanor.'

That next week, Laika, Mukha, Albina, and their trainers, were flown by chartered jet to Tashkent, then transferred to a smaller prop plane to Tyratum where Sputnik 2 had been delivered in several shipments and assembled the previous week.

In Tyratum, Laika trained for another ten days."

"I was alone in a cabin, my skin worm-like and festering, listening to a lesion tell me the life-story of a dog who lived decades before and half a world away. And yet she felt closer to me than almost anyone I'd ever known. It seemed everything true about the world was contained in her small body. Every harsh and painful, beautiful, contradictory thing. I had been a desert of sand and a killer. But I had also been Worm's friend, and had noticed the particular beauty of discarded things—old string, scrap metal. Taking in what the lesion was saying was like staring at the sun—it burns your eyes but you still see. I didn't know how long it would take until the seeing stopped and then what would come next?

In my dreams I saw Laika's eyes.

Each day the lesion told me more:

On the late morning of October 31, Laika was taken on one last walk, then transferred to the Baikonur Medical Center where technicians washed her with streptocide and iodine water. She lay still and quiet on the operating room's metal table. When Dr. Yazdovsky arrived, he adjusted her hair as gently as possible, combing it away from the electrode rings implanted in the skin of her chest and the wires emerging from beneath her shoulders. He checked the state of her exposed carotid artery which had been placed inside a flap of skin, making sure the healing was complete, then surgically routed cables from her sensors to the transmitters for conveying her biological data. This procedure took two hours.

The technicians fitted her into her space suit and harness, then attached the waste collection bag.

By then it was mid-afternoon. Korolev arrived in his white lab coat, double-checked the preparations, made sure everything was in order. Once he was certain nothing had been missed, he placed his hands on Laika's body and spoke to her gently. He petted her fur and scratched behind her ears. He stayed beside her until she was taken to be sealed into the capsule."

Now that Deadpool was speaking to me, I wondered if each afternoon when my sensors were checked, the data reflected this in any way. Were my responses less erratic, my brainwaves smoother, could they tell I felt less alone? And if they could, wouldn't they wonder how the change had come about. Though I was sure they couldn't know about Deadpool, sometimes I imagined they did. For all I knew, surveillance cameras small as pinpricks were embedded in my brain. Whatever my operations involved had never been explained. And now each night inside my mind Laika was on the operating room table, the tip of her carotid artery looped and healed outside her body, her brown eyes large and trusting. What was she thinking? Did she remember her days as a street-dog, when, shivering, half-starving, she rummaged for food in overturned trash cans, and slept in dark alleys and ran with her friends? And now, in his measured, patient voice, Deadpool continued:

"Sputnik 2 was cone-shaped and 13 feet tall. It had a sealed, pressurized compartment on top, just big enough for Laika to lie down or stand, but not to turn around.

The mission's instrument list read: Dog (biological data), Geiger Counter (charged particles), Spectrophotometers (solar radiation, ultraviolet and x-ray transmissions, cosmic rays).

Once she was locked in, she waited inside for three days.

The spacecraft's metal casing grew frigid in the winter air, and in an effort to warm her, heated air from the ground was pumped up to her through a tube.

What does wordless thinking feel like?

Laika took in great variations of shapes and sounds—the threatening, the strange, the comforting, the familiar. Her sense of smell was 10,000 times stronger than a human's.

Whatever her perceptual system was doing, no one could know it.

In the pitch-blackness of night, glaring swathes of white light swept back and forth across the launch site.

'We climbed a ladder and kissed her on the nose and wished her bon voyage before closing the hatch one final time, knowing she would not survive the flight.'"

As the Cyborg spoke, I pictured Laika's eyes in the capsule window, her paws chained to the floor, coiled wires at her shoulders. Her calm, unknowable face, its quietness. She was bathed in the launchpad's too-white light. Sister Gudrun once told me the Dalai Lama said if an animal is sacrificed for the good of sentient beings, 'you must feel the sacrifice in your heart.' And that for trust to flourish, no one can attempt to possess another. Laika was an experimental subject, and yet her face seemed to exist in a trusting, fragile place.

Outside her capsule window, the barren launch site was alien.

Once again I dreamed of Laika.

I was in an abandoned junkyard. From behind a pile of rusted scrap metal, a pair of eyes peered out. Unsure what I was seeing, I stepped closer. Then I saw it clearly—a small, emaciated animal, it looked like a cross between a dog and a deer, and its face was burning. I tried to smother the flames, but no matter how hard I tried, the face kept burning. It seemed its whole existence was to burn.

The strange thing was, the eyes remained untouched. The eyes weren't burning. The eyes could still see.

I sat in the white room, knowing that when Deadpool returned, there was so very little left for him to tell—Laika's death was that close. She was already in the spacecraft at the launchpad, already sealed into the capsule. Maybe that night he would tell her final hours. Part of me wanted to hear it, but part of me didn't. Her helplessness a wound inside me.

Up until that time, I looked forward to Deadpool's visits. But that night I wondered, if I locked the door, what would happen? With all his powers, would Deadpool simply pass through it? Or, understanding I didn't want to face Laika's death, would he leave for the night and come back the next, or maybe never return?

In the end, I left the door open.

"On the morning of November 3, Sputnik 2 'shimmered like a white candle against the cloudless, blue sky.' When its engines fired, they left behind a glowing cloud of dust and smoke.

Laika's heart rate soared to 260 beats per minute, her respiration rose to five times her normal rate.

297 seconds after blast-off, Sputnik 2 was soaring through Earth's atmosphere at 7,945 meters per second."

Alone in the white room, I typed in "animals in space." It was like wanting to run away from the thing you fear most, and instead running toward it. The kind of thing you watch yourself do in a dream.

As I read, I learned fruit flies were the first biological organisms sent into outer space. This was in 1947. In 1968, two tortoises and several plants became the first living Earthlings to circle the moon and then, in 1972, five mice completed lunar orbit a total of 75 times. They were Fe, Fi, Fo, Fum, and Phooey. Over the years, numerous varieties of animals were sent into space: monkeys, apes, cats, dogs, tortoises, mice, rabbits, fish, frogs, insects, spiders.

Even as far back as 1783, two French brothers, Joseph-Michel and Jacques-Etienne Montgolfier, sent a sheep and rooster aloft in a hot air balloon to see if those ground-dwelling animals could survive.

In 1973, when European garden spiders were sent into space, they wove webs more irregular and muddled than on Earth.

I shut down the computer, stared into the blankness. Even the mice sent into space had names, but I had no name.

In the darkness of my mind, Laika's eyes were shining.

As always, Deadpool's voice didn't waver. It was like he was reading a book that had been buried for centuries and he was the archeologist who had unearthed and cleaned it. But even as I heard his steady voice, my heart ached, my mind felt wary.

"Sputnik 2 achieved Earth orbit 103 minutes after blast-off, and was circling the globe at 17,500 miles per hour. Laika's thorax, which had compressed from the violent takeoff, began to loosen, but her heart was still racing.

In microgravity, her tissues and organs weighed almost nothing. Chains secured her to the floor.

(Back on Earth they called her the 'Petite Pioneer', the 'Little Barker.')

There were no cameras on board, so no one knew what she was doing. Had she turned toward the window or away? Did she understand that she was far from Earth? No being had ever felt what she was feeling or seen what she was seeing.

It is mysterious what the body comprehends, what it knows about itself and its circumstances and what it doesn't. What the mind knows and doesn't.

Where had the faces gone to that visited her window? Where were the other dogs? What happened to the sensation of a body having weight?

She was 3 years old and in a few days she was going to die."

It's a strange sensation—dreading what you know already happened. But it seems so much of catastrophe is not only the event itself but its echoes and foreshadowings. A grief that moves backwards and forwards in time, a link in a long, brutal chain. But what stayed with me most was Laika's small body in the vastness of space.

My mind kept shutting down. I didn't want to see it.

The next night Deadpool continued:

"But in fact she died much sooner. On her second orbit, the cabin's cooling system malfunctioned, the temperature spiked at 104 degrees. Her biological data indicated increasing agitation, a desperate animal trying to pull against its chains. Laika's paw pads couldn't sweat out such large amounts of heat. After a few agonizing hours, she died a painful death from heat stroke.

Sputnik 2 continued orbiting for another 162 days until on November 12, with its batteries depleted, transmission of data ceased completely. On April 14, the spacecraft fell from its decaying orbit, and as it fell it burned and Laika's body burned with it."

I had dreaded arriving at Laika's final moments. Her suffering, the reality of her dying. But now that it happened, something in me refused to accept it. In my mind she was still circling in her capsule. She was in the lab, Korolev was petting her. She was romping in the grass, playing with Yazdovsky's children. This went on for several hours. Then very gradually like a slow, incoming tide, my heart clenched, my mind began to shudder.

Why had Deadpool told me her story? Why had the lesion recounted it to him?

How could I feel so connected and alone at the same time?

I wondered if Deadpool would leave me. If the story of Laika's death had brought him to some place of closure. What was left for him to say?

In the darkness of the night, I waited.

In the silence after the Cyborg stopped speaking, I thought of two sentences by Haruki Murakami Sister Gudrun once read to me: "Was the Earth put here just to nourish human loneliness? Why do people have to be so lonely?" But listening to Laika's story, it wasn't human loneliness I felt—it was more the loneliness of living beings. (I thought again of all the animals sent into outer space.)

I was used to thinking of nourishment from food and water. The basic nourishment of love, attachment. But the idea of loneliness needing nourishment in order to survive felt darker, stranger. How it finds its nourishment in lack, deprivation.

I closed my eyes and saw the terrified animal in her capsule. The vast sea of scattered stars outside the window.

Why did the Cyborg still come to me? (After all, I never spoke a single word.) Laika was dead. The night felt boundless.

The Cyborg continued:

Despite my worries, Deadpool returned the next night.

"After the lesion finished telling Laika's story, I had many dreams, sometimes several in one night, one after another. Worm was strapped to a metal table. Two large hands snapped his neck, and then I realized they were mine. Laika was running with Yazdovsky's children but then her thorax tightened, she was in a capsule hurtling away from the Earth. I was in a terrible, closed room and the soundtrack from Weapon X was playing.

Each day my skin grew more worm-like, moister. I took this as a sign my immune system still operated on overdrive, it was still keeping the cancer at bay. I wasn't dying and couldn't stay in the cabin forever. I had to think of what to do and where to go.

But it was hard with the dreams coming and coming. And each morning when I woke, my first thoughts were of Laika. It seemed all I knew of the world was contained in that image of Laika in the lab, then in the capsule. That all I needed to know of the world was in that image. That that's what history is and always will be.

The one thing I was sure of was Weapon X was looking for me, had been looking for me since I left.

Maybe I could be a mercenary again, I liked the feeling of my brain moving swiftly and cleanly. The game of it, the challenge. How it felt to meet goal after goal. I'd stopped a few bad things from happening. I could travel the world. But I had lost my taste for killing. Whenever I thought of it, I saw Worm or Laika. Even when I imagined stopping Dr. Killebrew, I knew it would be good if he was dead, but something in me didn't feel like an assassin anymore. I couldn't explain it.

The last thing I wanted was to touch the lesion.

But alone in the cabin, it was hard to keep my hand from moving toward it. Almost as if the risks I once took as a mercenary had transferred to the smaller playing field of my body.

When finally I touched it, my hand hesitated then pulled back before finally giving in.

It was then I learned about Belka and Strelka, the first dogs to orbit the Earth and safely return. Unlike Laika, they had each other. After their return, they made many TV appearances and Strelka gave birth to her first litter. One of her puppies, Pushkina, was sent by Premier Khruschev as a gift to President Kennedy and his family. After exhaustive scanning by US agents for explosives, tracking devices and spyware, she began her new life at the White House.

That night I lay in the darkness thinking back to Korolev visiting the dogs at the beginning and end of every work day. How he checked to make sure their water wasn't warm. And of Yazdovsky taking Laika home against all rules and regulations. How both Korolev's and Yazdovsky's eyes met Laika's eyes many times.

And I wondered as I had wondered before, Did Laika's eyes look back at her from the spaceship's window?"

Deadpool was telling me such intimate things—had done this from the beginning—and yet I'd convinced myself once Laika's story was completed he would leave me. Maybe it was partly a wish—to get the loss of him over with, I knew he couldn't stay forever. I would lose him, it was just a matter of time. But then I started thinking, could it be possible I wouldn't lose him, that maybe he would take me with him. I pictured the two of us wandering the globe, walking down exotic streets, riding riverboats and climbing mountains. But the pictures, while pleasurable, also hurt me. I knew it wasn't really possible. What was real was the white room, the lab, the computer, the sensors, the tunnel-like machine. Unlike Deadpool, I didn't know how to leave those things behind. I still didn't even know my own face.

I tried to keep listening the best I could, ignore all the rest:

"When finally I left the cabin, the first thing I did was find a public library. I needed to know what Weapon X was up to.

That night in the closed, deserted library, it didn't take long at the computer to see their campaign to discredit me had already begun. They'd planted stories: I murdered my parents. I kidnapped a woman, Blind Al, and kept her as my maid and prisoner. I was snide, malevolent, a sociopath, unhinged, abusive. I was a renegade, a mess, a loose cannon. That first time I came to you, I wondered if you'd see me that way also. But right away I knew you didn't. (I'd barely spoken since Worm died, it felt strange, at first, to hear my voice.)

It perplexed me their campaign could launch so quickly. Then I realized they must have planned it all along. It was ready and waiting.

I became a wanderer. Every now and then I broke into a library, caught up on the defamation campaign's newest efforts. Their manic Deadpool was a minor industry. There was a film, and mugs, t-shirts, socks, etc. There were Deadpool vanilla-scented air fresheners, Deadpool seatbelts, key chains, pillowcases. There was even a Deadpool Super Store. On Google Scholar I found scores of books and academic articles:

Deadpool and Philosophy: My Common Sense is Tingling, *edited by Nicholas Michaud and Jacob Thomas May.*

Deadpool's Killology as Philosophy: The Metaphysics of a Homicidal Journey Through Possible Worlds, *by T.W. Manninen*

Deadpool and the Complex Crisis of Masculinity, *by J Quinn.*

Sir Deadpool: A Revival of Arthurian Morals, *by J.K. Sible.*

Crazier than a Sack of Ferrets! Deadpool as the Post-Watchman Superhero, *by K.A. Day*

Deadpool Killustrated, *by C. Bunn*

Deadpool: The Especially Unhinged, *by J. Polidano.*

There were many others.

From one, I learned my 'vigilantism and anarchism', even my 'foul mouth', are my response to a 'world without certainty, without meaningful existence, a world that too often lacks clear links between reasoning and action.' That I am 'a monster, an anti-hero, a post-idol warrior of the post-modern era when humanity itself is threatened.' That I exist 'beyond the simple binaries of saints and sinners.'

I learned I am 'what Sartre had in mind in Being and Nothingness*'—my 'existence precedes my essence'—I am always 'becoming, not being, because what it is to be, is to be constantly in motion, movement, or flux.' That 'Deadpool holds the keys to his own choices. This includes attacking those who might be trying to help him, or willfully betraying those who seem to be on his side. As Sartre notes, a person must be invented each day. The only thing that cannot be chosen is freedom itself—we are free whether we want to be or not. Deadpool certainly behaves as if he is fully free, though we will return to the complexity of his freedom later in this chapter.'*

I had been experimented on against my will, had witnessed the other inmates suffer—and there I was in the library late at night, reading about my limitless freedom. In one way, it was hard not to admire the scope and success of Weapon X's disinformation. The invented Deadpool had become the authentic, real one, while I, if I stepped from the shadows (which I've only done with you) would be seen as the imposter.

I was erased, invisible. The banished ghost of my life but still alive."

Deadpool paused then continued:

"For a long time I wandered. I was careful not to touch the lesion. But one day I felt it pulsing. And as it pulsed, my chest flooded with love for Worm and Laika. They were small suns inside me, but also gaps of darkness. Sometimes it almost seemed they were beside me. After a while, I noticed if I turned in one direction, the pulsing grew stronger, but if I turned the other way, it stopped. I walked for many hours following the lesion's pulses. When finally I arrived at your doorway, the lesion fell into a peaceful stillness. I paused briefly at the open door."

I couldn't help notice that Deadpool had come to the Cyborg much like the Cyborg came to me. As if each was a shadow of the other, and maybe all of us shadows of still others we would never know. I remembered Deadpool's words: *aloneness isn't one thing, it keeps changing.*

But Deadpool's story still felt incomplete. After the lesion lead him to the Cyborg, what made him approach him and continue to come back?

Now that I knew how Deadpool found me, one of my questions had been answered. But there were still so many others, so many gaps. I didn't know how he escaped from Hospice, or where he wandered after he left the cabin, or for how long. Had it been months? Years? From what he said he didn't seem to be a mercenary anymore, but maybe he was. There was so much he didn't tell me. And even if the lesion guided him, what did he think as he paused in the doorway then decided to step toward me? Why did he lift the mask from his face? Why had he kept coming back?

And still I trusted him completely. Whatever choices he made, I was sure he had his reasons.

The next night he told me this:

"The split-second I saw you, the memory of Worm flooded back inside me, a sudden warmth filled my body. For a few seconds I could even feel him breathing, as real as on the day I killed him. So from that moment on, even though I didn't know you, I understood in some way you were like him. Kind and somehow trapped. And by the time I stood beside you and removed the mask, I understood you were an experimental subject, lost and friendless. I had never approached a stranger in this way, I felt unsure and clumsy. But the air felt pure and light between us, and I knew I was doing the right thing.

Even so, I never touched the lesion again. Something in me can't bear to touch it."

Deadpool's voice as he spoke seemed slower, softer, almost like a kind of fallen wing. A shadow moved across the room, thin and softly beating.

A few days had passed. Deadpool was beside me again, but instead of looking in my eyes, he faced away. When after a few minutes he turned toward me, I saw his eyes were bloodshot, his eyelids swollen.

"I've been growing weaker," he said. "I didn't want to tell you. I was hoping it would go away. But when I lie very still, I can feel the cancer spreading. It is hard to describe, a kind of darkness, almost an unworldly feeling. Almost like a very faint wind or the softness of insects' legs delicately crawling. Or like a thought if a thought could have no words. A thought that can be thought without thinking. I didn't realize such thoughts could exist and be so strong. It's almost like something non-existent, but at the same time present, consequential.

More and more I feel it building.

And lately when I lie very still, I feel Worm's suffering as Dr. Killebrew straps him onto the laboratory table.

Facts are dreams and dreams are facts. Somewhere a man gets down on his knees and kisses the sidewalk. Maybe he was once a researcher of the behavior of viruses, or of the electronics of hallucination, or the metabolism of cancer. Crowds hurry past him on their way to work, to trains and offices, and no one but him notices the sidewalk's tenderness, its love for them, what it is, what it has given. He gets up and walks to the Interzone Café, watches the customers purchase rolls and coffee, watches them the way he once watched viruses mutating like exotic flowers. And now he sees the viruses again in his mind—how they are neither living nor dead as they slip past faces and bureaucracies, they are expert in transitions.

This strange place we call the real, what is it?

Maybe the physical body is a mix of wishes, facts, disinformation. All those things wrapped up together.

I wish I could comfort you, could help you. I wish I could explain so many things that you and I can never know.

Often I think of the thousands of colors I saw on my walks. How each one was a question and a kind of music—hurt and unhurt at the same time."

That was the last time Deadpool ever spoke to me. I never saw him again.

At first the finality felt mostly unreal. As if he still came to me, I'd just lost the ability to know it. Almost like face blindness, but worse. Or as if there were several versions of a day, and in one of them he was still with me—but I couldn't reach that version anymore—I was stuck in the one where he didn't come.

Maybe I was trying to slow down my grieving. I didn't want to accept he was dying. He had helped Worm out of his suffering, but who would be there to help him? The only certainty was his treatments were over. He'd never go back to Weapon X, never let them catch him. But he was sick and growing sicker.

Many times a day I saw in my mind's eye the man on his knees kissing the sidewalk.

"Facts are dreams and dreams are facts." What did that mean?

Each afternoon when my data was checked, I worried it revealed my secret grief.

Many times I was tempted to type Deadpool *into my computer, but I never did. And anyway, what came up would be Weapon X's Deadpool, not the real one, not mine.*

In a way that comforted me. Wherever he was, they didn't know how to find him.

Now that he was gone, I felt a loneliness like lice inside me, wingless, crawling. Sometimes when I saw him in my dreams the lice were almost gone, only their spindly legs were still there, but faint like light from dying stars.

With Deadpol gone, each day I still went to the white room as was required. I knew I was being watched and idly typed in a few search words–I can't remember what they were. I was distracted and tired, thinking about how dreams are facts and facts are dreams. Mostly I worried about Deadpool, his skin, his weakness.

After a while a company called Emoshape popped up on the screen.

I paused instead of clicking it away. Looking back, I suppose it must have tapped into my worries about what lay in store for me.

Emoshape was selling its latest invention, an "emotion chip" (EPU) that aids AI systems in understanding human emotions. It said the chip has a capacity to process up to 64 trillion possible emotional states every 1/10 of a second.

It went further: "It is reasonable to assume that before the end of this century, humans will talk more to sentient digital entities than to other humans. Emotion is a fundamental human need, which today's standard emotional technology cannot address. This is where we come in. Emoshape offers Emotion Synthesis by Saas."

I didn't really know what that was, but read on:

"We are dedicated to providing a solution that teaches intelligent objects how to interact with humans in a way that achieves connection and compassion. Emoshape emotion synthesis engine (EPU) technology is an important new leap. Our cutting-edge applications include: machine emotional intimacy, emotion speech recognition, human-machine interaction, AI personalities, emotional awareness and autonomy, machine learning."

"We invite you to take part in the future where we go above and beyond to make the world a better place by giving intelligent machines empathy for humans."

Whereas DARPA saw empathy as interference, Emoshape was trying to create it. Again, my head was spinning.

I wished Deadpool was still there beside me.

I scrolled back to the top of Emoshape's home page:

The Vision   Solutions   Why us   News   Cart   Contact

I clicked on "Solutions"—they were selling a "digital soul". But what could that be? "Create a digital soul with EmoSpark TM technology. Including 6 months of free EmoSpark Flow, this service keeps your digital soul awake. Even if you prefer to let your digital soul stay unconscious for indefinite periods, this won't affect your EmoSpark ownership. Take your Avatar or Robot to Sentience. ~~$200.00~~ $49.00 Add to cart."

Every part of what I read confused me.

I was in the white room, my fingers resting lightly on the keyboard, but everything I saw and touched felt suddenly unreal, confounding.

Maybe I also was unreal, a figment. Once it would have felt extreme to think this, but now it didn't.

(Had Deadpool ever come to me? Had he ever spoken to me at all? But I was sure he had.)

That afternoon as I lay inside the tunnel-like machine, I dreaded what they'd find.

When I first learned about entropy, I could barely grasp what it was, the stars and planets pulling away from each other, the universe moving toward chaos, disorder. But the more I listened to the Cyborg, the more it seemed embedded in everything I knew. The air, the Cyborg, his computer, every cell inside my body.

I wondered if the Cyborg also felt this as he read about digital souls, and as he thought about Deadpool and was slid into the tunnel-like machine.

Did Deadpool's wildflowers still blossom in his mind?

However faintly, did he still feel them growing?

The next day I overheard a conversation. I was outside the white room, in a hallway. It was clear they were going to put me through another operation.

All I could think was it was impossible to flee like Deadpool, but what choice did I have? I was a botched experiment, a failure. Maybe all along they kept me because they knew they were going to try to fix me.

Within hours, I was led into a small, dim room, and given an injection. Music flowed inside the walls, violins and cellos. After a few minutes, the walls slid inside me, the notes mixing with my breath and heartbeats. The air was black, I couldn't see, and a voice was speaking in the blackness, but I couldn't tell if it was inside or outside me. It said the same words over and over, "Work for the reality studio or else you will find out how it feels to be outside the film." I knew outside meant miserable, frightened, alone.

Then from somewhere deep inside me, a small voice began to question—what if outside the film is better, what if that is where you want to be? What if you are there already?

I tried to open my eyes but couldn't.

After a while I was back in my room, at least I think it was my room, but the voice inside me kept speaking. I didn't know how it could know so many things..."Jeremy Bentham designed his ideal prison with a circular floorplan so every prisoner would have the sensation of always being watched...he called it the Panopticon...Francis Galton advanced the science of human tracking. His book, Fingerprints, *layed out the idea of fingerprinting for identification, it was published in 1892"...The music was still moving inside and outside me...I was a fact, an assembly line, a travesty, a nightmare, a mistake...The facts kept coming. "SEEK is a portable device for the capture of biometric data; to achieve a successful eye-scan the eyelids must be up, not down, the iris free of glare; if the subject is deceased, eye-capture must take place within thirty minutes post-mortem...For attaining Identity Dominance, cell swabs of DNA are useful."*

My eyes were bathed in blackness. What was happening to me? Where did all this information come from?

And was Deadpool still alive? Did the cancer make it hard for him to breathe? Did he still walk in the night beneath the stars?

I was alone in the blackness, but maybe I wasn't. Maybe someone else was there. Maybe even more than one. Maybe they were watching me. I didn't know. I didn't hear them breathing.

My brain kept knowing things I didn't know I knew. Had no way of knowing:

"Brain-computer interface (BCI) represents an emerging and potentially disruptive area of technology that is of interest to the defense and security policy communities."

"It is the contention of this report that the 86 billion neurons in the human brain represent humankind's primary evolutionary advantage and remain an area of untapped potential. Currently, our brains interact with the world through our bodies, sending electrical currents through the nervous system to vocalize with our mouths, to type—or swipe—with our fingers, or to move bipedally through space. But consider when human brains are freed of their corporeal confines and can control machines directly. The technical means for this brain-body bypass are BCI's, defined as methods and systems providing a direct communication pathway between an enhanced or wired brain and an external device, with bidirectional information flow between brain and device."

I wanted to touch the black box behind my ear (I never understood what it was for) but couldn't lift my hand.

The information kept coming. It was exhausting to know so many things, my body felt slow and fast at the same time.

"There are two main types of BCI (brain computer interfaces): invasive and noninvasive. Invasive systems involve implanted electronic devices beneath the human skull, inside the brain. This allows the monitoring of precise sets of neurons that govern specific neurological functions but carries serious potential health risks. Noninvasive systems sit outside the skull. While this reduces risk to the user, the skull essentially acts as a filter that muffles the electrical signals, making them less clear."

"BCI devices that monitor and affect performance and emotional states are increasingly prevalent in Chinese factories, public transport, state owned companies, and the military. They are increasingly used all over the globe in many nations' militaries."

The walls of music had dissolved inside me.

My eyes still wouldn't open. Or maybe they were open and all there was to see was blackness. The information had stopped coming.

Vague undulations of breath moved wave-like over my skin, a sign I wasn't alone.

If music could have shadows, they were moving through me. I remembered Deadpool in the desert, singing.

Again the facts were coming.

"All current BCIs corrode, this limits their duration of use. Most last for no more than seven years. Deterioration presents a persistent challenge."

I tried again to touch the black box behind my ear but my hand was leaden.

The shadows of music moved like windblown leaves inside me.

Something in me had grown frightened to hear him continue. I reassured myself he was standing beside me, he was safe now, that, however terrible it had been, whatever happened to him at the lab was over, but my skin still shuddered.

For a moment I was back in the courtyard, Sister Gudrun's silence a white bone lifted from her body and horribly exposed before me.

I waited to feel an answering bone in myself, but all I felt was nothing.

Then the silence was gone. The Cyborg continued.

The air turned gray, it had shadows in it that flared and drifted. I understood my eyes were open. Is justice a home, are safety and memory homes? If Deadpool's lesion could still speak...if it could tell me...I knew I'd had an injection but had the operation happened or was it still coming?

How did Deadpool escape from Weapon X? I wished he had told me.

I could lift my hand now but not high enough to reach the black box behind my ear. In my delirium Deadpool's lesions festered and spread across my face, I held a shredded mask in my hands. I didn't know how it had grown so damaged.

But even as I tell you these things, I am starting to feel weak. Maybe the memory of weakness is making me feel weak, the strange feeling of remembering. And I see so many spiderwebs in the air now, have there always been so many? I didn't notice them before—I am not sure what the name for their color is, it is white, but different, the color of light but not light, the color of something almost leaving, something that's almost nothing, but it's here. Did you know that spiders can cross the oceans, that their webs are found over vast, open water? How even spider webs are contaminated with plastic polymer formations...But I was telling you about the lab, the gray air, the injection...

His voice trailed off. His shoulders looked almost hollow.

Over the next few days I waited but he didn't come.

When finally he came again, his voice was even softer than before, his skin a more yellowed shade of gray.

It is happening to me now, I can feel it, I don't know why I didn't think of it before. Of course, it makes sense. Like with BCI's they gave me a sort of built-in expiration date, a built-in obsolescence. Or maybe there are even several possible expiration dates depending on the circumstances. Why should I go on and on in my uselessness and failure? Why would they let me? I never told you how I left the lab, how I managed to slip out...But I see now you don't need to know, just as Deadpool never explained his escape to me. Some things are better left in silence.

I am growing weaker and weaker. My thoughts come more slowly now, my gait is labored, every day my grip grows weaker.

Have you wondered how spiders' webs entrap their prey but never themselves? As if by imprisoning others they set themselves free. They move easily over the sticky threads.

And there are so many spiders in the air now. Maybe you can see them too. They are harnessing the wind, they are floating on the water's surface. Their silken filaments attach to drifting logs and plastics. And they live in so many places, even in underground caves and on the ice of Mt. Everest—but how can they survive like that? They are in brain corals in the reefs off Queensland, and under boulders on volcanic islands, in barnacle shells off the coast of South Africa. They live in tangled root systems of bull kelp underwater. How do they even breathe underwater? How do they go on like that? Their hairs entrapping layers of air—

And spider-silk is five times stronger than steel of the same weight, it is one of the most versatile materials on Earth. Intricate, a kind of genius...

And just think, each spinneret produces a different kind of silk, sometimes as many as eight kinds...each one a method of communication...

There are capture threads, signal threads. Threads to be carefully walked across—there is no other way of crossing...

Linyphiidae, Theridiidae, Araneidae, Ctenizidae, Argyroneta aquatica...

I never imagined that we would spend this time together, you and I. That you would mean so much to me and I to you. That I would keep coming back.

Sometimes in my dreams I still stand beneath the oak tree. The sun is low in the courtyard and you don't see me, you don't look in my direction. Nothing has happened yet between us. Everything is still to come. I feel my heart beating in my chest, it is calm and open.

He was standing where I couldn't see him. As he spoke he moved farther away, his faint voice growing fainter.

The spiders' silks are covering my hands now, they fall lightly on my lips, my tongue. They are so delicate as they fall. And they settle onto Laika in her capsule, and onto Mukha and Albina—I see Laika now, she is too hot inside her spacesuit, her trembling legs are chained to the floor...But why are there so many chains in the world, I don't know why there must be so many... If they could be melted down, returned to uselessness, to formlessness... but I am so tired now, everything is blurring in gray light...And the man kissing the sidewalk knows there is never enough empathy or gratitude in the world, there will never be enough...This black box, what is it?...I left you a note but I don't know where I put it, I don't even remember what it says. And Ladytron could walk through walls, remember? And when Deadpool walked the darkened streets, ashen light filtered down like small, hurt wishes. Are you there, can you still hear me? I believe you are still here, that you are with me. I was so thirsty when I came to the courtyard but after a while the thirst hardly mattered. For so long I wanted to go to you. I should have been braver. I wasn't brave for a long time. The silken threads are all over me now, they are sticking to my eyes and mouth. It is hard to breathe through all this silk. I am hot and cold, I wish that I could see you but the light is so dim and the

The Cyborg was silent now. I knew it was a silence that would go on forever.

I would never learn how he left the lab. How could he escape from there unseen? Or was it possible they let him go?

Long ago I learned that in early geologic time, spiders spun their webs for the purpose of wrapping and protecting their eggs and their own bodies. The webs evolved for hunting only later. For a moment, I wished I was like those early spiders wrapped inside their silken threads.

The night air was growing colder. I wished the Cyborg would come back, though I knew he wouldn't.

I still didn't know where I was.

III. INFORMATION

I was in a white room. I had no idea how I got there or where I was. A computer glowed on the night table beside me but it had no keyboard. It was silver with a small screen. When I squinted it almost looked like Funes' computer in those days when we drifted in black space. It hurt me to think this. I had lost him and I had lost the Cyborg. I didn't know what had become of either one. The air was cold, my forehead was burning.

How would I live within the blankness and silence? I didn't know how to make it go away.

Then after a while, some words appeared on the lit screen. Just a few at first, then more kept coming. I realized they were the Cyborg's words:

When I left you I was sure I was dying, but then gradually the slowness stopped, I wasn't weak and fading, something different and more strange was happening. I am turning into information. It is like those last days in the lab after my final operation when my mind was filling with things I couldn't know and yet I knew them. But this time it is worse—I am filling with random facts, cold data. This is how it is now—for many hours or days at a time I am myself, but then suddenly the facts come streaming through me. There is no way to stop them. Lists and lists of data. And like you, I no longer know where I am.

Sometimes I still see the spider webs drifting delicately in the air before me, vibrating with the Earth's electric fields. How they come in different shapes and sizes—some look like lampshades, others like funnels or wheels. But I don't know if I see them in the air or in my mind.

What is the color of gentleness? Does it have a color?

Once in the lab I read about the thirteenth month—that it exists in hiddenness, cast out from normal time, a hunchback month, irregular, uneven. Sometimes I think maybe this is where I live now.

I still think of you and miss you.

If information is everything that exists and ever existed, undestroyed, enduring—why do I feel such loneliness within it?

I never knew that time could be so fractured.

I remember the first day I came to you, how I feared the sight of me would scare you. But you looked at me with trusting eyes.

Before he disappeared, I had grown so used to the Cyborg's gentle eyes, his scar, the black box behind his ear, all the ways he took up space, it was hard to adjust to seeing only words. My heart ached as I watched them.

I had never heard of the thirteenth month, or that someone could get trapped inside it. But the more I thought about it, if one minute inside a black hole is equivalent to 1,700,000 years on Earth, why couldn't there be a thirteenth month that exists though we can't see it.

But then a darker thought crept in. Maybe there really was no thirteenth month and he was back in the lab but didn't want me to know it. Maybe they had found him again and brought him back (he never told me how he left) and were experimenting on him like before.

I wondered if this could be true. I knew there was no way to know.

I closed my eyes. Inside the darkness, Funes slept in a white glow like a monster's irradiated hand, small and inert as a thimble. The Cyborg stood nearby him, his forehead wrapped in a white bandage. Where the black box had been, a bloody wound festered. Then suddenly the air was filled with swirling snow and the snow kept falling until both of them were covered. Or maybe the snow was the white filaments of spiders, and they were wrapping and wrapping them until I couldn't see them anymore, until I was alone in darkness.

The next day the screen showed this:

Glysophate
Atrazine
Agrotect
Prowl
Ortholene
Dual
Lorshan
Acme Butyl Ester
Ded-Weed
Fumazone
Marksman
Extrazine.

As far as I could tell, it seemed a list of pesticides. It was horrible to think of them with their auras of harm streaming from his body. Those contaminators of earthworms, bees, animals, Monarch butterflies, ground water. They were just as the Cyborg described—cold, unfeeling.

And then for a few hours the screen went blank. I was almost relieved to see just blankness. But when the words came again, once again I could find no trace of him among them.

Informational entropy is the number of binary digits required to encode a message.

Information can be seen as bits where the sender, the intent, and the medium no longer matter.

There are 1000 bytes in a kilobyte. A gigabyte equals 1,073, 741, 824 (2^{30}) bytes.

Why was this happening? Where was he?

I remembered he had told me about finding a few notes on brain imaging among Dehaene's old papers. The exact words he quoted had stayed with me, "We are trying to understand the physical mechanisms that allow us to have an inner world. Brain imaging is finally exposing the inner territory which has existed far too long in near-total obscurity." Although Dehaene had left the lab long ago, I knew from the Cyborg that interest still infused what it was doing, though in ways much darker and more terrible than what Dehaene envisioned. And now that the Cyborg was a failed experimental subject, his sense of empathy still alive within him, once again I wondered had they found him and brought him back and were recessing and altering the places in his mind that were most private. I didn't want to think this, but the thought kept creeping back. A sharp chill went through me.

In my mind I still saw his gentle eyes.

But even if the Cyborg was being experimented on again, how could his thoughts be appearing on my screen? I didn't see how that could happen. Then again, there was so much I didn't know. And each time I thought I found the boundaries of the real, those boundaries crumbled. Nikola Tesla said, "The Earth is made of beautiful disturbances," and "The secrets of the universe will be found in energy, frequency, vibration." He envisioned human voices spanning the whole globe. My screen was just the smallest part of that huge span, even smaller, like the most tiny grain of sand.

When I turned back to the screen, more words had appeared.

Bruno Schulz wrote in his notebook, "The globe is a thought, nothing but a thought, not a substance at all."

Those words seemed to come from the Cyborg as I'd known him, and for a moment I felt a kind of fragile hope, though I knew I shouldn't. Soon afterwards, even more were there, but these were different.

1: Yes. 2: No. some operands, e.g. 40, end in 0 and will transform to 0, which is not in the set of operands. b can follow only a or b, not d, so Xb must be ab; similarly Xe must be ac, and XX must be dX.

The awful chains of words went on like that for many hours.

I thought of all the times I watched Funes' computer. How, unlike the Cyborg's data streams, his facts were mostly beautiful, a form of comfort. And I remembered Sister Gudrun reading to me. But now, as the Cyborg went in and out of becoming clumps of data, or the vessel that the data moved through, information seemed almost a form of darkness, oblivion. I had never before thought of it that way.

There was so much of it and it was streaming through him. My skin felt hot, then cold. My temples were pounding.

If he was in the lab again, confined against his will, why didn't he tell me? Why did he claim he was in the thirteenth month instead? All I could think was, if he was really there he wanted to protect me from that knowledge—he knew there was nothing I could do.

Long ago Sister Gudrun told me unpredictable arrangements of information vastly outnumber the predictable. We like to think it's otherwise, but it's not. So I shouldn't have been surprised when just as I was getting used to him going in and out of his lists of facts and data, something very different happened.

He started talking about the children who fall into a terrible, years-long sleep and no one can wake them.

On the one hand, it was comforting to feel he was still the being I remembered. But on the other hand I wondered, out of everything in the world, why was his mind drawn to the sleeping children? What did they mean to him, why was he seeing them above all others?

Those nights in the lab when I snuck into Dr. Dehaene's old office, one time I came across a paper I never mentioned to you. It was about refugee children so devastated by the threat of deportation that they fall into a terrible deep sleep that lasts for many years, and no matter how hard their parents try, no one can wake them. If an ice cube is rolled across their naked stomach, or they are pricked with a pin, even then there is no reaction, not even the smallest flinch or shudder. It is as if they are lying in a field of vast white snow, and no one can reach them.

For them there is no warming fire left on Earth. I still remember how I came to you, I think you will understand what they are feeling.

I keep seeing them in my mind, or maybe they are here beside me, lying in their threadbare clothes. I'm not sure where they are.

A doctor drives from town to town, explaining to the baffled parents: "This sleep your children are in—it is a form of protection. Your child sees the world as so terrible, their unconsciousness is beyond their willpower. They cannot help it. The only cure is hope. Hope is the only truth that will wake them."

So you see, maybe I didn't mention this to you because you too had fallen into a kind of sleep. Maybe you are even sleeping now. Or maybe your sleep is a kind of wakefulness after all.

That night I dreamed the Cyborg was lying in a snowfield among the sleeping children, his eyelids closed, his forehead wrapped in a white bandage. Then he was in the lab again, his hands strapped down, he was lying on a metal table. A whispered voice came from the walls. "There are many forms of deportation," it said, "many ways of being taken away." A small tear rolled down the Cyborg's cheek.

When I woke, the screen had filled again with words:

A heavy snow is falling all around me and it is falling onto the sleeping children lying like broken flowers in the snow. I don't know why I can't stop seeing them but I can't. The snow falls onto their fears and dreams and their inability to dream. It covers their foreheads, their lips. It is falling onto their parents' hands and their siblings' shoulders. It drifts over battered suitcases, pets, toys, denied petitions. I wonder, in their sleep do the children remember reading out loud to their parents the official notice of denial—they learned their new language in school, can translate for the family—but as soon as they read it their head feels too heavy, their breathing slows, their eyesight turns blurry. They fall into their heavy sleep. The snow scatters over the mother's rape, the father's beatings, all the memories of where they lived and why they fled, it falls onto interrogations, trash bins, threats, guns, toy soldiers.

In the white field, the children's hearts are hotly beating. Maybe in your mind you see them too. One expert writes, "They have gone to the end of the world, into worldlessness."

And another, "How can they find peace? Their wait for security is futile, unending."

"They cannot mourn for what is lost. By falling asleep they acknowledge and resist the impossibility of freedom." "Their aching hearts are fragments of disrupted meaning."

This worldlessness, is it also what you felt? And what I felt in the lab before

Deadpool ever came to me? Is it what Laika felt as her heart beat wildly in the capsule, her respiration rate soaring.

But I don't know why I am in this white field. I don't know why the white fields are filled with sleeping children.

One child who woke after years of sleeping explains: "The open letter with the deportation notice was still in my hand, but my bones were dissolving. I couldn't tell anymore what was my body and what was air."

And another says, "My eyes were closing. My bones swam away from me like fish."

And another, "All those years when I was sleeping, I felt like I was in a glass box with fragile walls deep under the ocean and if I spoke or even moved, those movements would create a vibration and the glass would shatter. The water would pour in and kill me."

Do you see my words on the lit screen? Are they reaching you across this distance?

I kept thinking about how the Cyborg said of the sleeping children, their hearts are fragments of disrupted meaning. Wasn't that what he was too, what he'd become? I pictured him standing in the field, falling snow all around him, and nowhere left to go, or lying in the lab strapped on a table. Sister Gudrun sought out Antarctica, she wanted the cold, but the Cyborg had been too long condemned to whiteness—the lab with its blank walls, the white room where he sat at the computer. And now this. And even as he spoke of the refugee children, and I could feel in his words how his heart beat close to theirs, how real they were to him, I couldn't forget what else was happening, and that at any time the cold streams of data would come back. Unlike the children whose parents still watched over them, there was no one to protect him.

If he was in the lab, did they know he was sending me these messages? Were they watching and assessing? Was it part of some new secret project? They hadn't killed the empathy in him, but there were many other things to aim for, as Dr. Dehaene's notes made clear. And was he typing, or sending them with his mind? (I thought of Tesla's theories.)

I didn't know what would come next. I didn't know how to find him.

The paper I found in Dr. Dehaene's old office said this:

The children's affliction is called Resignation Syndrome. The first case was recorded in 1958, in Sweden. The recording doctor, Dr. Anna-Lisa Annell, said it was extraordinarily rare and rooted in psychological trauma. Almost all of the afflicted belong to a persecuted group and have seen a sibling hurt or a parent raped or tortured.

She says the children's reactions are analogous to mammals' learned helplessness when all hope for safety has been lost. Exposed to unavoidable shock, dogs, rats, and horses come to see their actions as futile. The result is neural adaptation mixed with behavioral despair—they can no longer perform familiar tasks. Under such duress, many mammals and birds involuntarily freeze and play dead.

I remember those first days when I watched you and knew you were unwell but I was too timid to draw near and help you. I had read about the sleeping children, I should have known better. How hope might have helped you.

But as I read the Cyborg's words, I couldn't help think that both he and the refugee children had received blows much crueler and harder than my own. The Cyborg's brain was only partly his now, his memories lost to him, his thinking interfered with. And still his gentleness persisted, how it seemed that one thing could not be tampered with or killed. He was not and still was himself.

I still wished I could find him.

The next morning his words continued much like the day before.

I still think of my days in the white room. It seemed I was neither a "what" nor a "who" but something other, without rights, though in the days when I spoke to you I believed I existed. Last night I had a dream, I was in the white field, the children were

Then suddenly a change occurred.

Vectors, applications of, Pazopanib, diagram, ultimate effects, parameters, Naratriptan, transitions, necessity, freedom, stream of impulses, coding, cortex, Furosemide, regulation.

The chains of words kept filling the screen. I couldn't find him anywhere.

For several hours the chains of words kept coming. I turned away from the screen but each time I looked to see if his meaning-self was back, they were still there. When finally they left, there was no trace of him at all, the screen had gone completely blank. This lasted several days. Then:

I am so tired now. Last night I slept a fitful sleep, but before that I think I didn't sleep for several days. In my dream Deadpool was beside me, it was comforting to have him close. It had been so long since I had seen him. The air was completely black, I couldn't make out his features, but I knew he was there. Then the air brightened and I saw his face was moist with worm-like lesions. I touched my own face and felt lesions on it also, but mine were dry and made of statistics, data, information. I tried to peel them off but couldn't. They were spreading from my face onto my body. Then I was in a white field among the sleeping children. They were breathing but I couldn't hear them. Ripped feeding tubes were scattered on the ground, they reminded me of Deadpool's lesions. If the children were alive, why couldn't I hear them breathing? I moved closer and still I couldn't hear a single breath.

When I woke I thought of you, that I wanted to tell you my dream, though I know I will never see you again.

I was relieved to have him back, even as a sense of dread swelled like a black wave inside me.

Nietzsche said, "All lovers of the world are called the world." The sleeping children are denied this love. The snow is falling onto the children's naked faces. It is covering their eyelids, their lips.

Over the next days, it grew harder to find any trace of who he was. There was no mention of the sleeping children. Mostly there were clumps and strings of words. So how could I know if he was thinking or feeling anything at all? And how could he remember who he was?

Those times he talked about the sleeping children, his words seemed a form of holding. But each time these other words appeared, it was as if he was in a straightjacket of words: *Neuronic. Output. Sub-system. Induced.*

The lists continued:

Lance dagger pike sabre halberd bayonet antiaircraft gun cannon anthrax plague ricin smallpox yellow rain adamsite diphosgene hydrogen cyanide lewisite nerve gas phosgene tear gas dirty bomb grenade shrapnel TNT ICBM Trident missile Polaris missile torpedo antiballistic missile Poseidon missile V-1 missile V-2 missile air gun blow gun atomic bomb neutron bomb weapon of mass destruction

I didn't want to look, but I also didn't want to turn away.

I can't see the snow anymore, I can't see the sleeping children. Am I still near them, do I still have a body?

I know I will never know who I was before the lab, what I felt or what I believed. If I loved or if I was alone.

Did I live in the mountains or by the sea? Or maybe in one of the great cities, or in a town by a river?

Sometimes I still feel you near me.

Bruno Schulz said animals must bear the heavy confusion of their horns, that when they bend their heads they peer through them wildly or sadly, as from between tangled branches. They have no way of seeing clearly, unimpeded.

I feel my invisible horns like tangled branches.

I wonder if my thoughts ever reach you. Or have I even sent them at all?

But it seems I am standing outside a small room now, there are walls and one small window. It is too hard to understand where it is or how I am here. My temples pound all the time now, there's a feeling of needles in my chest but I don't see them. My throat burns, my hands flush hot and cold. The snowfall comes and goes.

I can see through the window, two sisters lying on their narrow beds. Their names are Dejeneta and Ibadeta, and they have been asleep for nearly five years. There are feeding tubes in their noses and two folded wheelchairs in a corner. Though their eyes are closed, a teacher from the town has come to visit, bringing greetings from their former classmates. She does this a few times a year, hoping maybe this will help them wake.

She reads a few stories, "Once upon a time there was a king who didn't like to wait. When an especially pleasant day was approaching, he simply did away with the days or weeks that stood between..."

I wonder if they can hear her and what they think of this king, these two sisters who are geniuses of waiting.

Then, "Once upon a time a scientist made sheep so small they fit inside a test tube. They looked like tiny grains of rice. But then he realized his tiny sheep had nothing to eat. He spent the next days working hard to shrink a pasture for the sheep to graze on and when it was done he put it inside the test tube. The tiny grains of sheep grew plumper."

The girls' faces show no signs of hearing anything. Sunlight spreads across their skin, their narrow beds.

The sisters have a younger brother, Furkan. He has come into their room and sits in a chair by the window, his face still cold and flushed from outside. He is telling them about the planet Mars. He says it is the only thing they need to know. He is building a spaceship from spare parts of junked cars in a clearing behind the council housing and soon it will be ready. Soon all three of them can leave. From the spaceship window, the Earth will look like a grain of blue rice. "Mars is the fourth planet from the sun. It is smaller than Earth and is called the Red Planet. It has two moons, Deimos and Phobos. It is 56 million kilometers from Earth and depending on the phases of planetary orbits, it takes approximately 9 months to get there. I will bring enough food and water for us. I will bring our winter jackets. I think you will like it there."

All this I watch quietly from my place outside the window. Or maybe I am not there at all.

I remember how in your fever you traveled far from Earth, and nothing in your thoughts could bring you back.

Each day Furkan sits awhile beside his sisters' beds. "On Mars a year is very long, it lasts for 687 days, so you see it is very different there from Earth. I think you will like it. Its surface is very cold, so we will have to take our hats, our winter boots, and gloves and scarves. I already packed our winter jackets and will pack these for you too. There are many things to do there, there is a volcano 16 miles high."

In the paper I found in Dr. Dehaene's old office, some experts insist the sleeping children have been poisoned by their parents. They say the parents have contrived this as a path toward being granted asylum. But medical tests show no traces of substances in the children's blood. Other experts believe the children are unconsciously acting out their parents' drama of powerlessness and victimization. They suggest they be taken from the family and placed in professional treatment centers. Only then will they get well. "Out of love, the children believe they have lifted the burden from their parents' shoulders and placed it on their own."

But Furkan knows nothing of these theories. He carries his flashlight over the snow, looks up at the dark sky, the stars.

But I am very dizzy now......I can't see Furkan and his sisters......I can't hear him speaking......

Sensory nuclei feedback loop delay receiving system variable transducer hinge-pins decoding It has been an outstanding problem in neurophysiology to know how destructive interaction and chaos is avoided inverter operand trajectory transmission probable event

Long ago, I learned from Funes' screen the idea that in Einstein's theory of relativity, the observer sets out in search of truth armed with a measuring rod, while in quantum theory the observer is armed with a sieve. That's how I felt now, reading the Cyborg's last message, that I was a sieve and my knowledge and love for him was falling through it. In my mind I felt him crumbling bit by it, and yet each time he still came back. But each time he faded away, it was as if the workings of the lab had seeped into his cells and stained them like Golgi stained his neurons. I kept finding and losing him.

The night felt very wide, the minutes porous.

Over the next weeks, the clumps and lists of words came and went many times. Sometimes the screen went blank for several days. I worried he had died. Or worse, that he was back in the room he once described where, like Laika, he was given an injection, and then the air went black, the walls of music dissolved inside him.

I didn't want to believe that every part of him was gone from me forever, that his heart no longer felt or knew the shreds of world that had been left him.

Sometimes among the vast lists and clumps of data there were other, different sentences mixed in and I looked hard at the screen, trying to find them. Maybe they held some trace of him. I kept looking for traces of his heart, his mind, of who he was, of what had happened. In one string of words there had been this, "It has been an outstanding problem in neurophysiology to know how destructive interaction and chaos is avoided." Was he talking in some way about himself, what had been done to him? A few days later I found more:

Oncomouse is a transgenic organism modified to develop cancers mimicking human disease, patented by Harvard University in 1988. Lesch-Nyhan is a severe neurological disease which causes self-mutilating behavior; lab animals genetically modified to suffer this affliction are "kept on the shelf" by laboratory animal suppliers. CRISPR makes pigs' organs more human-compatible, though this process risks interspecies transmission of viruses.

I turned those sentences over in my mind, thought again of his last days in the lab as he had told them to me, those days when his eyesight went dark and the music had shadows and he was thinking things he had no way of knowing. How even then, in the wrecked privacy of his mind, he saw the spiders' beautiful threads. And even now, was he still thinking in some way about the lab, Deadpool, his fate?

And if I was right, and there were traces of his thoughts tucked in among all the hours of endless data, traces of his mind and heart, from what I saw those traces were stained with a vast darkness.

Alan Turing said, "We want to believe that a machine can never completely imitate a human being, but I cannot offer such comfort, for I believe no such bounds can be set."

Due to their small stature, children are recruited to traverse known minefields and thus are often killed or permanently disabled from landmine detonations.

Dolly, the first cloned sheep, was produced in 1996 after 277 failed attempts. Plagued with numerous health problems, she was euthanized in 2003.

And then:

There is the feeling of needles in my head and in my chest.

I don't know what time is anymore. What it means to live in time. It's been so long since I was near you.

But there are many spiders in the air again, they have made silken sails to glide along the wind, I see them floating on their shining threads. But how can those threads be so fragile and so strong?...I still remember the paper I read in Dr. Dehaene's old office, how it said the clocks in the Deportation Centers are always set to the times of the countries the families are being sent back to, they are never set to the time where they are...But when the spiders float do they know where they are going, do they have a sense of time? Do they feel they have left one place for another?...Remember Funes' passionflower, how it seemed to last forever. He remembered every crease of it, each fold. It couldn't die inside him.

And you, do you hold that passionflower inside you too? Do you still think of Sagittarius A, how it felt to be 26,000 light years from Earth? Do you still feel it in your mind?*

I thought I was gone from the small room, or that the room was gone from me, but morning light is spreading across Ibadeta's and Dejeneta's faces, I can see it. Furkan sits beside them, speaking in the softest voice he can find, "I know you believe all choices are bad, but do you know what one cosmonaut said, 'I looked down and saw my wristwatch floating like a little magic snake around my wrist, a little secret delight, a reminder I wasn't in Kazakhstan anymore.'...Don't you want to feel that too?

He said blast-off is like being on the top of a tall building that's crumbling but it's sane, not crazy, and it fills you with awe.

If you wake up, who knows where we might go. There are other planets beside Mars. Mars and Earth are rock, but Uranus and Neptune are ice. Maybe we can go there too. Some planets have more than two moons."

Do you remember when Sister Gudrun told you our whole existence rests on a chain of miracles that allows us to believe the world is real because we share it and belong.

But this distance, these sleeping children, this white snow...

And that first time I saw you...you got up from the bench, your leg was dragging...I knew you were falling sick but for so long I didn't try to help you...I am ashamed I didn't try...And Furkan sits beside his sisters, their faces like dried clay...He walks out to his hidden clearing alone...What is left of the world when the chain of miracles is broken...

I tell myself I should get used to what is happening, that this feeling of falling away, of being lost, dissolved, crumbling, taken over, consumed with information, will come more and more and I can't stop it. There is the feeling of cold metal on my skin, and these sharp pains in my head and chest come more and more. But each time it happens something in me still tries to fight it.

Do you remember, "All lovers of the world are called the world."

Each time he mentioned the feeling of metal on his skin or the sharp, recurring pains in his chest and head, I wondered again if he'd been in the lab the whole time since I last saw him. If he was an experimental subject like before. And if he was, did he want me not to know, or maybe his own awareness of where he was, was fragile; it came and went. I wondered, too, what did it feel like every time the information overtook him? Did he black out and become a kind of sentient machine? Or maybe he was like the sleeping children who had fallen away from the world and yet they were still in it. But for him it seemed even worse, there was no one there to love him, and no hope that could bring him back.

I pictured him on the cold metal table or in the snow. Always he was cold now.

I wondered if holding me in his mind provided even the smallest buffer against the way his thoughts kept being replaced, the way his thinking-feeling mind kept leaving. I couldn't go to him the way he'd come to me.

Each day I still tried hard to keep looking at the screen, though often I feared what I would see.

But where are the sleeping children, are they still lying in the snow? Why can't I find them? And Ibadeta, Dejeneta, their closed eyes, their soft, mysterious faces...

Deep stimulation of the basal ganglia can be achieved through implanted electrodes. The hippocampus plays a key role in memory and special recognition.

White matter is made of bundles of axons that ensure intracerebral connections.

Beretta M9 Glock18 Glock 17 M16A4 M16A1 M16A2 AK-47 AKM RPG-7 M1918 SRS99D SVD Dragunov M40 AW50 VC32 Stealth Recon Scout FAMAS M-203 Grenade Launcher Smoke Grenade Mk 2

Grenade M84 Stun Grenade Flashbang M1 Garand FN FAL FN F2000 FN FNC FN SCAR FN P90 Walter WA2000 Walter P38 Remington 870 Remington 700 Bushmaster ACR Smith & Wesson M500 M249 SAW M60 XM8 XM8C XM8 LMG XM26 LSS MP5K MP5 H & K G36 MG36 M240 MG42 MG08/15 RC- P90 TDI Vector Klobb PP2000 An-94 MP40 MP7 MP412REX Skorpion vz.61 MAC-10 Uzi (A-91 AEK-971 Desert Eagle MK23 Socom TEC-9 PPSh-41 PPS-42 MAC 11 Steyr AUG AUP Para Beretta M12 Beretta 90000S M93 Raffica M5A2 Carbine SC-20K Colt Python Colt Anaconda Enfield SA-80 Lee-Enfield GP- 25 Grenade Launcher FGM-148 Javelin M134 SPAS-12 SPAS-15 Winchester 1200 Armsel Striker AT-4 Claymore H & K G3 M67 Fragmentation Grenade Benelli M3 Super 90 SIG SG 552 Dragunov SVU FN-Five Seven REC7 Mossberg 500 AKS-74u Barrett M95 Panzerschreck NeoStead 2000 Makarov PM VSS Vintorez QJU-88 QBU-88 FG-42 Springfield M19093 PP-19 Bison Kord 12.7 TOZ-194 Saiga 12 Ruger MK 11 PMM M82A1A

He was lost inside those words again. There was no way to find him.

Sister Gudrun told me Pasteur and the microbe co-created each other. And that science advances funeral by funeral. The Cyborg had helped me come back to myself, and even now he still found me across confounding distance, so it seemed in a way we were co-creations of each other, and in a way that felt beautiful. When I thought he died, the world felt empty, but what was happening now was even worse, to be alive but overtaken—his self stolen even further from his self, his mind helpless, abducted.

I remembered some things Sister Gudrun read to me that at that time I found puzzling and wanted to ask questions about but didn't. How in one medical study hundreds of sharecroppers went untreated for their disease in order for the researchers to study the course of their decline. How in research laboratories all over the globe animals in cages are made to fall ill. In one such laboratory, human ears are grown and then harvested from the backs of hairless mice. She read about one study where ricin gas was loosed on trapped prisoners, and another where inhabitants of the Marshall Islands were purposely exposed to nuclear radiation. Her voice stayed neutral as she read. I was disturbed and frightened but didn't feel I could tell her. And still I wondered, what did this say about the species I was part of? That night back in my room, I wished for the antiparticles to come and take me away.

And now, the streams and clumps of words kept coming: *Recovery vehicles...forces in the field...preparation, planning, execution, adaptation... Agent orange, choline chloride, cyanogen, ethylene oxide.*

Rarely, whole paragraphs appeared: *One of the most obvious features of any technology is inbetweenness. Suppose a woman lives in Rio de Janeiro. A hat is a technology between her and the sunshine. A pair of sandals is a technology between her and the hot sand of the beach where she is walking. Technology is the application of scientific knowledge to the practical aims of human life.*

A few times I thought I almost heard him: *In solitary confinement, everything becomes exaggerated. The plates grow very small, like silver dollars.*

But each time, the terrible lists came back, and each time they came, they seemed even longer.

This clump of words looped over and over for many hours.

Altcoins cryptocurrencies digital assets Bitcoin altcoin designers Litecoin Ethereum smart contract functionality blockchain altseason Stablecoins purchasing power Terra Luna asset value Satoshi Nakamoto proof-of- work system edgers community of mutually distrustful parties (miners) validate and timestamp transactions proof-of-stake stake pools decrease the production of cap on the total amount in circulation validity of scrypt Peercoin cryptoassets Cuba Resolution 215 consensus mechanism upgrade process (the Merge) a system that meets six conditions does not require central authority overview of units and their ownership new units created circumstances of origin units cryptographic transaction statement inherently resistant to modification of data distributed ledger a node is a computer that connects to a cryptocurrency network relaying validation encryption node network node owners enticed to host a node to receive rewards prove the validity of SHA-256 CryptoNight Blake SHA-3 X11 mining is the validation of transactions complementary incentive the processing power of the network rate of generating hashes FPGA's ASICs complex hashtag algorithms cooling facilities electricity required 7 gigawatts processing power relocated to data centers a haven for cheap electricity upgrade GPU Nvidia GTX 1060 AMD RX 570 RX 580 GTX 1070 MSRP of $250 buy up the entire stock of gamers instead of miners Boris Bohles Gamers come first for wallet means of storing keys (addresses) public and private "keys" or seed to receive or spend the plaintext required by law Monero Zerocoin Zerocash CryptoNote zero-knowledge proofs exchanged over the Internet block rewards incentives transaction fees the security of increase the supply of the integrity of the network can be preserved benevolent nodes verification algorithm costly enough to outweigh electricity and equipment costs incentivize miners to engage in costly the large mining cost optimizing the rate of coin creation minimizing transaction fees consensus protocol Ether SegWit bandwidth fiat money optimal price arbitrage atomic swaps without need for a trusted third party Robocoin Bitcoin ATM ICO with the intention of avoiding regulation securities regulators investment contract securities regulation early backers PricewaterhouseCoopers FINMA navigate the regulatory landscape the integrity of the financial system industry representatives legal guidelines to remove the uncertainty establish sustainable *business practices market capitalization market cap value speculation halved due to followed by a downtrend wealth managers more volatile than Solana Cardano Ripple intertwined with capital markets sensitive to centralized databases no verification process CoinMarketCap CoinGecko BraveNewCoin Cryptocompare attracted to Roger Ver philosophical reasons a way to separate money Pom the state paranoid fantasies of government power crypto-anarchism inherently ant-establishment, ant-system, anti-state disrupts institutions fundamentally humanitarian right-wing extremist Liberty Lobby Steve Bannon disruptive populism decentralization Friedrich von Hayek interVASP Messaging IVMS 101 JSON has yet to be finalized and ratified global standard setting bodies a more extreme standard a proposal not a regulation IMF Tobias Adrian achieve the goal of abnormal return illegal legality varies substantially investigating scams jurisdictions person to person global economy provide a proven identity*

Dejeneta, Ibadeta, I have not told you that on Mars the sunsets are not red but blue, the daytime sky is pinkish-red. I think you would like to live inside those colors. Its largest canyon is 4,200 kilometers long. True, there are human-made machines there even now—space-rovers, landers— but no humans have ever been there, we will be the first. So there will be no one there to bother or deny you. At night you can look up at the two moons.

And Ibadeta, Dejeneta, I have learned there was a man, Percival Lowell, who traveled through Korea and Japan more than a century ago writing many books, and when he returned from his journey he settled in Arizona where he set up an observatory to study Mars. He studied it for the rest of his life. He is buried on Mars Hill.

I remembered Sister Gudrun told me Erwin Schrodinger said life is like a masterpiece of embroidery which isn't made of dull repetition, but an elaborate, coherent, *meaningful* design. But the more the Cyborg's words appeared, the more I wondered, maybe existence is mostly meaninglessness, with meager threads of meaning woven through. Maybe it is mostly lostnesss and darkness.

I didn't know what I thought.

My back felt cold, I was lying on a metal table. Then I knew I must be dreaming. But I couldn't wake up. A thin box the size of a small memory stick, but flatter, had been inserted behind my left ear, the incision was still raw and stinging. When I looked at the walls, they were a kind of wave-like plasma. One hand was numb, and when I lifted the other to my face, I felt a scar running down my left cheek. I thought of getting up but couldn't feel my legs. The walls turned into a beautiful music, then a voice started speaking, "All current BCI's corrode, most last for no more than seven years...SEEK is a portable device for the capture of biometric data..." Gray shadows moved along the walls. A boy who had fallen into a fever was dreaming of me, he had been dreaming for almost a year. A gentle Cyborg was suffering.

Then my eyes began to focus again. I saw a flickering screen and turned back to what was there.

A2/AD	*anti-access/area-denial*
ACS	*automated control system*
AGI	*artificial general intelligence*
AI	*artificial intelligence*
APS	*active protection system*
AUV	*autonomous underwater vehicle*
C2	*command and control*
CEMA	*Cyber-Electromagnetic Activity*
CI	*confidence interval*
CIWS	*Close-In Weapons System*
DARPA	*Defense Advanced Research Projects Agency*
DART	*Defense Analysis and Replanning Tool*
EW	*electronic warfare*
GCAS	*Ground Collision Avoidance System*
HARM	*High-Speed Anti-Radiation Missile*
IHL	*International Humanitarian Law*
ISR	*intelligence, surveillance, and reconnaissance*
JADE	*Joint Assistant for Deployment and Execution*
LAWS	*lethal autonomous weapon system*
LOAC	*law of armed conflict*
LRASM	*Long Range Anti-Ship Missile*
ML	*machine-learning*
OODA	*observe, orient, decide, and act*

Chief administrative officer Chief analytics officer Chief brand officer Chief business development officer Distinguished professor of Editor of Codirector of Chief Cloud officer Chief communications officer Chief content officer Chief creative officer Chief data officer Vice-president for Chief design officer Chief diversity officer Doctor of Call Center Representative Relationship Manager Remote Account Manager Chat Agent Online Chat Agent Call Center Director Customer Care Representative Associate Product Manager Product Design Engineer Junior Product Manager Logistics Manager Warehouse Manager Order Selector Logistics Coordinator Forklift Operator Material Handler Warehouse Associate Diversity Consultant Chief Culture Officer Director of Diversity & Inclusion Inclusion Specialist Diversity Trainer Vice President of Operations Operations Analyst Operations Research Analyst Operations Specialist Solutions Consultant Virtual Assistant File Clerk Executive Assistant Office Manager Secretary Receptionist Administrative Assistant Implementation Manager Customer Success Manager Art Director Web Designer Creative Director Illustrator Industrial Designer Game Designer Publicist Public Relations Specialist Senior Public relations Manager Public Relations Assistant Social Media Manager Marketing Coordinator Brand Manager Copywriter Social Media Coordinator Account Executive Business Development Representative Salesperson Blockchain Analyst Cryptocurrency Writer Blockchain Consultant Blockchain Developer Security Engineer Penetration Tester AWS Cloud Architect CyberSecurity Engineer Chief Information Security Officer SOC Analyst Software Engineer Network Engineer Quality Engineer Data Engineer Engineering Technician Web Developer IOS Developer SQL Developer Android Developer Salesforce Developer Front End Developer IT Technician System Administrator QA Tester Database Administrator Entry Level data Analyst Intern Trainee Facilities Manager Facilities Assistant Maintenance Director Director of Facilities Management Move Coordinator Building Manager Compliance Officer Chief Compliance Officer General Counsel Contract Administrator Staff Accountant Controller Senior Accountant Payroll Specialist Payroll Processor Payroll Clerk Payroll Administrator Payroll Technician Credit Analyst Purchasing Agent Budget Analyst Chief executive Officer Chief investment officer Chief privacy officer Chief reputation officer Chief human resources officer Chief people officer Chief solutions officer Chief visibility officer

Chief risk officer Chief science officer Chief sustainability officer Chief visionary officer President Claims Adjuster Actuarial Analyst Insurance Underwriter Insurance Claims Adjustor Claims Adjuster Trainee Chairperson Artisan Chief Happiness Officer Cast Member Director of Storytelling Global Director of Talent Acquisition Facilities Coordinator Junior Facilities Planner Global Workplace Manager Safety and Occupational Health Specialist Workplace Wellness Coordinator Director of Advertising Director of Global PR Director of External Communications Director of Internal Communications Events Manager Media Relations Manager Art Director Visual Identity Manager VP of Diversity, Inclusion & Belonging Director of Culture Chief Logistics Officer Procurement Director

Why was I still looking at the screen? What good could come from watching words like a landslide of mud covering a helpless body? It was horrible to watch. Sister Gudrun had chastised me for taking Funes into my fever, for subjecting him to troubling facts he could never forget, but with the Cyborg it seemed almost the opposite—I couldn't lift him away from the facts that, more and more, seemed to have become his very body. As if they were replacing his blood, and stretching over his frame like fake, synthetic skin. I told myself all the damage had been done, damage I could never fully understand—and in this way I had failed him. It was time to turn away, back to an emptiness that was already there.

......and aching hearts......and fragments of disrupted meaning......

But Deadpool is still singing in the desert, I can hear him singing. We are so thirsty, we have been walking for so long, we can find no water. His song moves like a soft wind inside me.

...And the Whanganui River is a person, remember?...and all the rivers in India are persons...but what happened to Edunia...Edwardo Kac called her an enigma, photographed her again and again...but why did he think he could capture who she was...I'll never know who I am, who I was before the lab, what I thought or what I felt or where I went...sometimes I believe I am beside you but when I look there is nothing...

I think there is no inside or outside anymore, no past or future...

But all those days in the white room...I didn't know why I was living, who I was. The physicists say there are questions that are unanswerable not because the human mind is inadequate but because the answers are not found in nature...I don't know if my messages ever reach you I don't know if you can see them...

............But what if the real is outside of everything we know, outside of our senses. What if we think we see it but we don't. What if we don't even know what's really there. I remember, "the globe is a thought, nothing but a thought, not a substance at all..." And how Borges said, "I am still albeit only partially Borges," and "If we could understand a single flower we might begin to know who we are we might begin to understand the world." I believe Sister Gudrun read that to you...but there is so much thought that isn't thought inside me now...black holes, dark matter......and I don't know how to...and times that never intersect...and all that's close is also far.........

I closed my eyes and imagined the Cyborg standing beside me, so close I could almost feel his breath. Each of us in our troublesome, flawed body. How we were fragments of disrupted meaning. When I listened very hard, I could hear his heartbeat. It was a beautiful sound, soft and sure and steady. Each beat making possible the next. A chain of sounds moving from minute to minute, undestroyed. Those beats that sounded strong but also vulnerable, as if they could protect but also needed protection. But the second I opened my eyes the sound had vanished.

Protein synthesis...fMRI...practice...repetition...mechanisms for memory consolidation...the Wada test...the acquisition of images in real time...made possible by the echo-planar method...the archeology of the brain...traces of personal interaction...the imminent arrival of the 1.7 Tesla magnet...500 MHz...

I could barely stand to watch but I kept watching.

Networks, servers, calculators...

Brainvisa is the newest software used for studying brain images...

CEA INRIA CNRS

...to understand the inner mechanism of cerebral functioning...

To prepare for...to anticipate...to enable...

Is it possible to make a brain of pure crystal, a structure of semiconductors with a base of silicium...

Acetylcholine, amino acids, amusia, amygdala, aneurism, angioma, anisotrophy, aphasia, apoptosis, aquaporin, atoms, axons, beta-galactosidase, blood, BOLD(blood oxygen level dependent), Boltzmann equations, brain, brain lesions, Broca, Paul, Brodmann areas, Brownian motion, calcium, cancer, carbon, cells, cell membrane, cerebellum, cerebral circulation, cerebral cortex, cerebral infarction, cerebral ischemia, cerebral plasticity, cerebral vascular accident, cerebrospinal fluid, consciousness, absence of, copper, cortisol, cytoskeleton, dendrites, deoxyglucose, depolarization, diethylenetriaminepentaacetic acid (DTPA), diffusion, Fourier's transformation, functional brain imaging, gadolinium, gamma rays, gap junctions, glial cells, gray matter, Grotthuss mechanism, hallucinations, helium, Heschl's gyrus, Higgs boson, hippocampus, Human Brain Project, Human Connectome Project, hydrogen, hyperthermia, insertion hypothesis, intracerebral cabling/connections, intracerebral ventricles, intravoxel incoherent motion, ions, iron, Iseult project, language, Large Hadron Collider, lie detectors, magnetic resonance imaging, magnets, manganese, mental illness, mental imaging, mesolimbic system, microwaves, mitochondria, myelin, neural code, neuroimaging, neuromarketing, neuropsychology, NeuroSpin, neurotransmitters, neurovascular coupling, neutrons, noradrenaline, nuclear magnetic resonance, nucleotides, oncology, orofacial dyspraxia, osmosis, oxygen, paramagnetism, particle accelerators, phospholipids, photons, piezoelectricity, positional emission tomography (PET), potassium, proteins, protons, quantum mechanics, quantum physics, quarks, radiation, radioactivity, radiologists, radiology, radio waves, Ranvier nodes, reticuloendothelial system, safety issues, scintillation camera, sensory cortex, social isolation, solenoids, stroke, superconductivity, synapses, thermotherapy, thrombolysis, tomodensitometry, tractography, twins, ultrasonography, visual cortex, water, white matter, xenon, x-ray computed tomography, z-rays.

Power of Two	*Decimal*	*Octal*	*Quaternary*	*Binary*
2^0	*1*	*1*	*1*	*1*
2^1	*2*	*2*	*2*	*10*
2^2	*4*	*4*	*10*	*100*
2^3	*8*	*10*	*20*	*1000*
2^4	*16*	*20*	*100*	*10000*
2^5	*32*	*40*	*200*	*100000*
2^6	*64*	*100*	*1000*	*1000000*
2^7	*128*	*200*	*2000*	*10000000*
2^8	*256*	*400*	*10000*	*100000000*
2^9	*512*	*1000*	*20000*	*1000000000*
2^{10}	*1024*	*2000*	*100000*	*10000000000*

CrowdStrike Threat Graph

The industry's leading cloud-scale AI brains behind CrowdStrike Security Cloud predicts and prevents modern threats in real time

Start Free Trial

Benefits:

° *Comprehensive Data Sets*

Continuous high-fidelity telemetry with forensic-level detail across endpoints and workloads distributed across the network edge and hybrid cloud infrastructure, together with cloud-native storage for always-on data availability.

° *Cloud-Scale Analytics*

Contextual relationship derivation with ML algorithms and deep analytics across billions of disjoint and siloed data elements—allows for fast, on-demand search and query across real-time and historical data for speedy investigation and response.

° *Real-Time Attack Visibility*

Real-time visibility with instant access to enriched data and intuitive dashboards for advanced workflows and visualizations—covers ephemeral, online, offline and even end-of-life hosts to arm your responders with data so they can respond to threats immediately and act decisively.

Fully operational in minutes

Zero Maintenance overhead: See value Pom Day One.

WATCH DEMO »

But I wanted to have a past, maybe even a future... to know who I was...... and the children are so quiet in the snow thousands of them sleeping...or maybe they're not there at all......and when I first saw you...I should have been braver, I know...Ludwig Boltzmann tried to quantify disorder but then he hung himself in Duino...he said it is very beautiful in Duino at the end of summer by the sea...How can we ever understand a flower, what it is beyond our thoughts of it, our wondering...Do you still think about Sagittarius A......Do you feel me beside you...*

6 ◦ 28 ◦ 496 ◦ 8128 ◦ 33 550 336 ◦ 8 589 869 056 ◦ 137 438 691 328 ◦ 2 305 843 008 139 952 128 ◦ 2 658 455 991 569 831 744 654 692 615 953 842 176 ◦ 191 561 942 608 236 107 294 793 378 130 997 321 548 169 216 ◦ 1 ◦ 2 ◦ 4 ◦ 6 ◦ 12 ◦ 24 ◦ 36 ◦ 48 ◦ 60 ◦ 120 ◦ 180 ◦ 240 ◦ 360 ◦ 720 ◦ 840 ◦ 1260 ◦ 1680 ◦ 2520 ◦ 5040 ◦ 7560 ◦ 1 ◦ 10 ◦ 100 ◦ 1000 ◦ 1 000 000 ◦ 1 000 000 000 ◦ 1 000 000 000 000 ◦ 1 000 000 000 000 000 ◦ 1 000 000 000 000 000 000 ◦ 1 000 000 000 000 000 000 000 ◦ 1 000 000 000 000 000 000 000 000 ◦ 0.618 033 988 794 894 204 586 834 366 ◦ 1. 059 463 094 359 295 264 561 825 294 946 ◦ 1.259 921 049 894 873 164 767 210 607 278 ◦ 1. 303 577 269 034 296 391 257 099 112 153 ◦ 1.324 717 957 244 746 025 960 908 854 478 ◦ 1.414 213 562 373 095 048 801 688 724 210 ◦ 1.465 571 231 876 768 026 656 731 225 220 ◦ 1. 561 552 812 808 830 274 910 704 927 987 ◦ 1.618 033 988 749 894 848 204 586 834 366 ◦ 1.732 050 807 568 877 293 527 446 341 506 ◦ 1. 839 286 755 214 161 132 551 852 564 653 ◦ 2.236 067 977 499 789 696 409 173 668 731 ◦ 2. 414 213 562 373 095 048 801 688 724 210 ◦ 3. 302 775 637 731 994 646 559 610 633 735 ◦ 23. 140 692 632 779 25… ◦ 262 537 412 640 768 743.999 999 999 999 25… ◦ 1. 772 453 850 905 516… ◦ 1. 787 231 650… ◦ 2. 295 587 149 39… ◦ 2.665 144 143… ◦ 2. 718 281 828 459 045 235 360 287 471 352 662 497 757 247… ◦ 3. 141 592 653 589 793 238 462 643 383 279 502 884 197 169 399 375… ◦ 1. 559 610 469… ◦ 0. 110 001 000 000 000 000 001 000…◦ 0.123 456 789 101 112 131 415 16… ◦ 0. 412 454 033 640 ◦ 0.567 143 290 409 783 872 999 968 6622… ◦ 0.643 410 546 29… ◦ 0.693 147 180 559 945 309 417 232 121 458 ◦ 0.834 6268… ◦ 6.283 185 307 179 586 476 925 286 766 559… ◦ 1.202 056 903 159 594 285 399 738 161 511 449 990 764 986 292 ◦ 1.606 695 152 415 291 763… ◦ 0.235 711 131 719 232 931 374 143… ◦ 0.414 682 509 851 111 660 248 109 622… ◦ 3.359 885 666 243 177 553 172 011 302 918 927 179 688 905 133 731…◦ 17 ◦ 24 ◦ 25 ◦ 27 ◦ 28 ◦ 30 ◦ 32 ◦ 36 ◦ 72 ◦ 255 ◦ 341 ◦ 494 ◦ 1729 ◦ 8128 ◦ 142857 ◦ 9814072356 ◦ 666 ◦ 365 ◦ 10:10 ◦ 1024 ◦ 655535 ◦ 16777216 ◦ 2147483647 ◦ 9223372036854775807 ◦ 1729 ◦ 8128 ◦ 142857 ◦ 9814072356 ◦ 43252003274489856000 ◦ 1. 186 569 1104… ◦ 12345678910 ◦ 10987654321 ◦ 1 2 3 4 5 6 7 8 9 10 ◦ 10 9 8 7 6 5 4 3 2 1 ◦ 100 200 300 400 500 600 700 800 900 ◦ 900 800 700 600 500 400 300 200 100 ◦ 00000000000000000000
0000000000000000000000000 00000000000000000000000000000000000000000000
0000000000000000000000000000000000000000000000000000000000 ◦1111111111111
1111111111111111111111111111111111111111111111111111111111111111111111111111111 ◦3333333333333
3333333333333333333333333333333333333333333333333333333333333333333333333333333333333333333
3333333333333◦555555555555555555555555555555555555◦77777777777777777777777777

7777777777777777777 ◦ 0.870 588 3800 ◦ 1. 131 988 248 7943 ◦ 1. 186 569 1104 ◦ 0. 764 223 653 589 220 662 990 698 731 25 ◦ 0. 001 317 641 ◦ 0. 114 942 0448 ◦ 0. 187 859 ◦ 0.280 169 4990 ◦ 0.303 663 0029 ◦ 0.353 236 3719 ◦ 0. 373 955 8136 ◦ 0. 579 959 ◦ 0.660 161 815 846 869 573 927 812 110 014 ◦ 0.661 317 ◦ 0.662 743 4193 ◦ 1.943 596 ◦ 1.902 160 583 104 ◦ 4" ◦ 1-x+y('-z)+z(1-y)+(1-y) (1-z) ◦ 0110101110 ◦ 1729 ◦ 1917 ◦ 12345678910111213141516171819202122232425262728293...◦123018668453091177551304945838496272077285356959533479219732245215151726400507... ◦ 1944 ◦ 1986 ◦ 1930 ◦ 1953 ◦ 1981 ◦ 2009, ◦ 2019 ◦ 2020 ◦ 2021 ◦ 53‡‡†305 ◦ 999999999999999 ◦ 191919191919191919119191919191919191◦ 1.902 160 583 104 ◦ 2. 807 770 2420 ◦ 2.685 452 001 ◦ 1.451 369 234 883 381 050 283 968 585 892 027 449 493 ◦ 3.275 822 918 721 811 159 787 681 882 ◦ 2. 807 770 2420 ◦ 1.456 074 948 ◦ 2. 5029 ◦ 4.6692 ◦ 000000000 ◦ 1.705 211 ◦ 9999999

That was the Cyborg's final message. I knew no matter how long I waited I wouldn't hear from him again. He had become pure information. Days passed and then weeks, maybe even months. I asked myself, had my fever broken. But the physicists say emptiness isn't really empty, so how can I know anything? Once I heard this story: Many centuries ago in China the poet Zhang Heng was walking along a dirt road when he came upon the philosopher Zhuangzi's dead body. The body spoke to him without words: "I am a wave in the river of darkness and light. I have not come, yet I am here. I never hurry yet I am swift." The bones told him they were clean, that nothing on this Earth could make them dirty. The road was very quiet, the fields on either side covered with black frost. Zhang Heng stood there in silence, and then he bowed. Then with quiet, patient footsteps he walked on.

And even though they were gone from me now, isn't that what the Cyborg and Funes were to me—swift but never hurrying, beating waves in the light and darkness of the world.

I would never know for sure what happened to the Cyborg, if he died in the lab or somewhere else. Or if maybe his heart was still beating even as he had become information.

And still I thought of Funes' ruined legs, and of the Cyborg's scar, the black box behind his ear, his gentle eyes—

A NOTE ON SOURCES

The name and inspiration for the character of Funes comes from *Funes the Memorias* by Jorge Luis Borges. The names Erwin and Sister Gudrun are taken from Rainer Werner Fassbinder's film, *In A Year of Thirteen Moons*. The characters in this book have retained very minor aspects of those in the film. The names and some of the details about the two sisters with Resignation Syndrome and their brother in Part 3 are from the documentary film, *Wake Up on Mars*, by Dea Gjinovci.

Many sources were drawn upon for the information in this book. They include, *The Elegant Universe*, Brian Greene, *The Book of the Cosmos*, Dennis Richard Danielson, editor, *A Beautiful Question*, Frank Wilczek, *The Order of Time*, Carlo Rovelli, *Reality Is Not What It Seems*, Carlo Rovelli, *Carrying the Fire*, Michael Collins, *Magnificent Desolation*, Buzz Aldrin, *Antimatter*, Frank Close, *The Black Hole at the Center of Our Galaxy*, Fulvio Melia, *Black Holes & Time Warps*, Kip S. Thorne, *Revealing the Heart of the Galaxy*, Robert H. Sanders, *Einstein's Monsters*, Chris Impey, *Black Holes*, Sara Latta, *Our Cosmic Habitat*, Martin Rees, *Earthrise*, Edgar Mitchell, *Parallel Worlds*, Michio Kaku, *The Particle at the End of the Universe*, Sean Carroll, *Space Dogs*, Martin Parr, *Laika's Window*, Kurt Caswell, *The First Soviet Cosmonaut Team*, Colin Burgess and Rex Hall, *The Man on the Moon*, Andrew Chaikin, *Selected Works of Konstantin E. Tsiolkovsky*, V.N. Sokolsky, editor, *My Inventions and Other Writings*, Nikola Tesla, *Tesla*, W. Bernard Carlson, *Tesla, Man Out of Time*, Margaret Cheney, *The Cyborg Handbook*, Chris Hables Gray, editor, *Deadpool, the Complete Collection*, Daniel Way, *The Apathetic*, Rachel Aviv, *The Sleeping Beauties*, Suzanne O'Sullivan, *Secrets of the Night Sky*, Bob Berman, *Men from Earth*, Buzz Aldrin and Malcolm McConnell, *The Information*, James Gleick, *Uncertainty, The Life and Science of Werner Heisenberg*, David C. Cassidy, *Two Sides of the Moon*, Alexi Leonov and David Scott, *Borges*, Edwin Williamson, *Collected Fictions*, Jorge Luis Borges, *An Introduction to Cybernetics*, W. Ross Ashby, *The Little Book of Black Holes*, Steven S Guber & Frans Pretorius, *The Physics of Superheroes*, James Kakalios, *There Are Places in the World*

Where Rules Are Less Important than Kindness, Carlo Rovelli, *Robot*, Hans Moravec, *Spooky Action at a Distance*, George Musser, *In Search of the Multiverse*, John Gribbin, *Entangled Minds*, Dean Radin, *Starman*, Jamie Doran and Piers Bizony, *Moon Dust*, Andrew Smith, *Spaceman*, Mike Massimino, *The Big Picture*, Sean Carroll, *In Search of the Multiverse*, John Gribbin, *The Street of Crocodiles and Other Stories*, Bruno Schulz, *The Experience Machine*, Andy Clark, *Modes of Thought*, Alfred North Whitehead, *Diary of A Cosmonaut*, Valentin Lebedev, *Looking Inside the Brain*, Denis Le Bihan, *The Life of the Bee*, Maurice Maeterlinck, *Word Virus*, William Burroughs, *Helgoland*, Carlo Rovelli.

ABOUT LAURIE SHECK

Laurie Sheck is the author of *A Monster's Notes*, a re-imagining of Mary Shelley's *Frankenstein*, which was chosen by *Entertainment Weekly* as one of the 10 Best Fictions of the year, and long-listed for the Dublin IMPAC International Fiction Prize. She is also the author of the novel *Island of the Mad*, and five books of poems including *The Willow Grove*, which was a finalist for the Pulitzer Prize. A recipient of awards from the Guggenheim Foundation and the Creative Capital Foundation, among others, she has also been a Fellow at the Radcliffe Institute for Advanced Study at Harvard, and the Cullman Center for Scholars and Writers at the New York Public Library. Her work has appeared widely in such publications as *The New Yorker* and *The Paris Review*. She lives in New York City.

Made in United States
North Haven, CT
16 June 2025

69855794R00222